A CHANCE ENCOUNTER

What's a cuff link doing on the cement floor under a gas hood? Good question. What were the odds of a cuff link being there? Slim to none.

Then I looked around a bench and saw a rather large piece of this probability puzzle. It kind of completed the picture.

Lying on his back, staring me in the face, was the block of wood I'd seen at Apollo's. Only he was no longer digesting his crumbling bacon and medium eggs.

I screamed, backed off, hit my head on something, and toppled over backward. I crawled toward the door, jumped up, grabbed the knob, turned it, and raced out of Mindy Sayles's loft, out of the building, out of my skin. . . .

Also by Bob Berger

Beating Murphy's Law

THE DR. RISK DETECTIVE SERIES

The Risk
of
Murder

BOB BERGER

A Dell Book

Published by
Dell Publishing
a division of
Bantam Doubleday Dell Publishing Group, Inc.
1540 Broadway
New York, New York 10036

ISBN: 0-440-22051-3

Printed in the United States of America

Published simultaneously in Canada

November 1995

10 9 8 7 6 5 4 3 2 1

OPM

To E.R. and S.C., for taking the risk.

To Howard Warshaw, Laurel Terry, Lee Berger,
Nancy Yost, and Marjorie Braman

"Proof," [Philip Marlowe] said, "is always a relative thing. It's an overwhelming balance of probabilities."

—Raymond Chandler
Farewell, My Lovely

"In the long run, we are all dead."

—John Maynard Keynes

CHAPTER
1

I bet it's every guy's dream to live for just a second in the gumshoes of Philip Marlowe or James Bond. To be as tough as nails yet cashmere casual. To sucker-punch the bad guy and in the same motion flick a Bic at the lady's cigarette.

Sure, it's a fantasy. Hard-nosed, rough as a five o'clock shadow, whiskey-slurping, heart of gold . . . in this age of political correctness, men like that no longer exist. (And maybe they shouldn't. And maybe they never did.)

But a little birdie whispers alluringly to me, "That's you, bud, if you just took a chance."

I don't . . . take chances. My name is Dr. Risk. I predict risky events and try to avoid them. I write a biweekly newspaper column discussing the dangers of drinking milk, the greenhouse effect, using a condom, and, of course, not using a condom, eating linguine. You name it, I know how risky it is.

But I don't get myself into risky situations. I stay away from danger, past, present, and future tense.

I'm not a wimp. I study tai chi with my little Taoist master, P. K. Chan. Tai chi, if you're unaware, lets you dispose of enemies without strength, anger, or sweat. It's as close to risk-free in the martial arts as you get.

Sarah, my fiancée, loves my disposition. She thinks life's risky enough, especially with Keri around; Keri's her six-year-old from a previous marriage.

Risk theory is an odd science, a catchall of disciplines. Before getting into it, I wrote journalism, programmed software, worked in the stock market, and even accompanied a singer on a piano through a whole lot of Ramada Inns. All these skills require a small affinity to math and a large affinity to being a jack-of-all-trades.

Then one day I helped my lawyer friend Buzz Howard win a rape case. Using probability theory in those early days of DNA testing, when accuracy was a lot smaller, I pioneered a way to combine several different blood tests to free a retarded Jamaican immigrant who'd been railroaded by the police into confessing. (The actual rapist was later found and convicted.)

The case made *The New York Times* and *News-*

week. In fact, with *Newsweek* calling me "an expert in risk theory," lawyers and environmental groups started phoning me around the clock. With lots of moxie, plus an ancient knowledge of chemistry, an ability to fiddle expertly with a spreadsheet, and a determination to get my hands on tons of statistics, my career began.

I'm now established, though I continue to work out of my tiny office in the basement of the Greenwich Village building where I keep an apartment. On my bright red rocker I seesaw up to everything here; the microwave in the corner, the fridge, my CD, the toilet in the foyer, Mad Max, my IBM clone. It may sound claustrophobic, but I don't have to move around much here to get at my stuff, and that's efficient. And efficiency diminishes risk.

What does a risk theorist do? Lots of things. I'm up for an incinerator assessment assignment—say that quickly, I dare you—for the City of New York. I recently made *The New York Times* by correctly predicting—I missed by five—how many murders would occur in the past six months in New York City (I based my calculations on ammunition sold in the tristate area).

Plus I figure out "factoids." Right now I'm finding the average number of bees in a beehive for an insurance company. Believe it or not, the insurance company is fighting the lawsuit of a very unlucky picnicker who got fatally stung about two thousand times (meaning two thousand New England honeybees; bees are kamikaze, diving onto your flight deck and dropping dead while letting you have it). Insurance covered only a single hive. Was two thousand full occupancy?

To find this, I used Mad Max to search through the Internet—I live or die by the Internet—to ask several expert apiarists (beekeepers) with their own news group to post me their estimates. After several did, I averaged the bees, after subtracting the estimates of drone bees, which don't sting, and faxed back my standard contract, demanding in this case two hundred dollars. Now, that may sound meager, but three or four "factoids" like this a week can free up lots of time for golf.

I rarely leave my office. Clients fax or E-mail me here. I hardly even speak on the phone. Though I've worked with clients as big as IBM (and as small as the corner grocer: Hakim wanted to know the odds of winning the lottery; I charged him a buttered bagel), I'm a faceless, voiceless anonymity to most. Dr. Risk, who takes no risks.

And I'm sick of that. I didn't get into this to avoid risks, or become a man who worries instead of acts.

In short, I was not living my life. I was reading detective novels. It wasn't healthy.

And then the phone rang and changed my life.

My answering machine screened it. "Dr. Risk?" I heard after my recorded message. A woman's voice. I picked up the receiver.

"Yes?"

"My name's Mindy. Sayles," the voice said.

"I'm a sculptor. I live in TriBeCa. Sarah gave me your number."

Ah, a friend of Sarah's. A gold-plated recommendation. "What can I do for you, Ms. Sayles?"

"We have to meet."

I thought for a second. "About what?"

"Can't tell you now," Mindy Sayles said. "But I have to meet you."

"So many women say that . . ." I wished. "How about tomorrow?"

"I have to see you now. Please!"

I heard something on the phone, a clicking. Too rhythmic to be static, it sounded like a machine. "How about the Apollo?" I said.

"Apollo?"

"Not the one in Harlem. It's a diner off Sheridan Square. Greenwich Village."

"I'll be there in fifteen minutes," Mindy Sayles said breathlessly, and hung up, leaving me to stare at the phone for a clue to what would happen next.

Nothing happened next. Nothing risky. I put Mad Max on doze and got my Yankee cap.

CHAPTER
2

Outside I ran into the loveliest spring day, the kind that makes you actually like New York City. Blue sky, nothing but blue sky. Greenwich Village is one neighborhood where you can see sky. A yellow sun spit-polished fenders and sooty windshields, as I nodded to the statue of General Sheridan, the Civil War hero, in the park across the street. Philip Sheridan, sculpted in a kind of indignant outrage, stares past pigeon turds in his mustache at what in his day would have been labeled the sins of Beelzebub. Sheridan Square, you see, is the symbolic dead center of gay USA.

Philip, smile. Times have changed.

I sprinted across Seventh Avenue near the square. About six or seven streets intersect here, so you'd better sprint; it's risky coming and going. I bought a paper from Nehru, my Indian newspaper guy in the outdoor kiosk, and crossed a tiny misplaced part of Grove Street ten feet in front of a fiery tourist bus. I entered the safety of the Apollo Diner with a sigh.

And then I realized I hadn't a clue what this woman looked like. Well, Dr. Risk, what were the odds she'd be a beauty, a fabled 10?

I guess at odds and risks to pass the time. Sherlock Holmes could look at your shoes and figure if you came from Hampshire or Haverford. I can look at your shoe and tell you the odds of its being size six (and thus the odds of your being below average height or weight).

Let's figure the odds of Mindy Sayles's being a beauty. First clue? Her voice. Nasal. Arid. Unsexy. The odds tilt toward unattractive.

Second clue. She was a sculptor. Sculptors, I'll assume, tend to be strong, strong hands, masculine features.

The odds of a sculptor's being a raving beauty? A whole lot slimmer than one in ten.

Being head bookie here, I predict nineteen to one against a raving knock-out. One dollar gets you twenty. Any takers?

You should have bet. A long shot was walking in the door.

"I'm Mindy Sayles," said a truly beautiful redhead with azure blue eyes, ruby lips, full, beautiful breasts . . .

"Oh," I said and coughed. "And I'm James Denny." I shook her hand. Mindy stared at me a moment. " 'Dr. Risk' is a pseudonym, Mindy. My editor made me."

Mindy stared some more.

"Uh, it's a pleasure to meet you," I added as she sat down in the booth.

I ordered coffee from Michael, who had suddenly appeared, forever-smiling Michael Apollonius, whose smile today stretched inches farther. "Brush your teeth, Michael?" I said, frowning.

"You want tea?" he said, smile disappearing, and left.

"You're some hit." I motioned to two waiters, a short-order cook, and the man in the booth across the way, all staring as if to memorize her shade of lipstick. Mindy shrugged. For all she cared, they might have been blocks of wood.

But I was Dr. Risk.

Michael reappeared and, with his usual élan, dropped two cups of coffee from a height of about two feet. One day he'll scald me to death. "Ready to order?" he said, panting.

"Uh, excuse me, I've been waiting," said the block of wood across in the booth.

I looked at Michael. He looked at me.

"I'll have two medium eggs," the guy said, trying to look over my shoulder at Mindy and not succeeding, "over easy. Not browned, okay? I hate browned."

Michael watched steadfastly, then scribbled like a maniac.

"Rye toast, butter on the side, lightly toasted, no burn marks, okay?" he continued.

"Sure," Michael said, huffing.

"French fries, not home fries. It's too late for home fries."

"They get better," Michael ventured.

The block of wood glared. "Baloney. And I don't want baloney. I want bacon. Burnt. So it crumbles in my fingers."

Michael, the consummate pro, nodded. He turned back to us.

"Hungry?" I asked Mindy.

"Not anymore."

"Toast," I said to Michael. "Toasted," I added with a wink. Michael raced off.

"Boy," Mindy Sayles whispered to me, gesturing toward the block of wood, "I've never heard breakfast ordered like that."

"Then the odds are you're new in town."

Mindy squinted. "How'd you know?"

"New Yorkers, who think they're all gourmets, order their breakfasts in Greek diners like they're detailing a ten-course banquet at Lutèce. They particularize their Belgian waffles and sausage with the complexity of several stanzas of Urdu poetry."

"That's funny," Mindy Sayles said. But she didn't smile.

"How do you know Sarah?" I asked.

"Her advertising company wanted a mock-up for an ad. We don't know each other well."

"All right. How can I help you?"

Mindy shrugged. I nodded. She nodded. I shrugged. At this rate we'd leave our booth with lots of cricks in our necks. "Mindy, do you know what I do?" Mindy nodded again. I didn't believe her. "I write a column popularizing risk theory. I E-mail professors in Texas about binomial coefficients. I find and calculate different risks."

"I want to find a risk."

"Good. We're in the same ballpark."

Silence from Mindy.

"Mindy, I'm no good at grilling my clients. I rarely even meet my clients."

"Okay," Mindy said. "This isn't . . . God, I feel stupid. Mr. Denny, I'm an artist, but I don't think in terms of beauty. For instance, you look handsome . . ."

"Me?"

Mindy Sayles leaned forward. I'd recently read a study on body language and the probabilities of lying. If you lean forward, it's likely you're lying.

"It's what's behind the appearance that counts," she continued. "And something bad is behind it. Very bad."

I hadn't a clue what was going on, so I stared in the mirror next to the table to explore my possible handsomeness. I spotted a youthful-looking forty-one-year-old man with a strong chin, blue eyes, full, sensual lips . . . a receding hairline . . . an excess of nose hair . . .

Sarah tells me I'm handsome. Sarah is wined and dined to tell me that.

"Toast," Michael cried, returning and dropping two dishes on the table to startle me back into consciousness. Mindy buttered a piece for herself.

"That slab of butter will slice fifteen minutes off your life," I said with ghoulish humor, to kid her out of her thoughts of "something bad."

"Come on!" she cried through a mouthful.

"Only if you put on extra weight and keep it on," I said, laughing. I'd done a risk assessment equating extra calories to loss of life expectancy.

"I've read your column," she said, chewing. "I liked it. The photo makes you look older."

I've complained forever about that by-line photo. They want me looking older. Older and wiser.

"Actually the real reason I called," Mindy Sayles said, then stopped and looked down, "is that I think I'm being followed."

"Followed?"

"I think someone's after me right now."

There was a loud report, almost an explosion. I nearly flew out of the seat.

Our neighbor, the block of wood, inspected the pieces of saucer that had just smashed and scattered on the tile floor.

"Why don't you," I muttered, nervously settling back into the booth, "call the police?"

"I did, a few times. No one came. They . . . may be involved."

"The police?" I cried.

"I'm not making this up."

I'm sure she wasn't. But why tell me? Risk theory doesn't teach you how to lose a tail. "Perhaps the police screwed up," I said. "The average IQ at the police academy is probably below average."

"They didn't screw up. Something is wrong, Mr. Denny. I need you," Mindy Sayles said.

It's very nice to be needed, especially by someone as pretty as Mindy Sayles.

"You see, I just got into town," she said. "I don't have a family, and I haven't made many friends, so I don't know who to trust." She looked at her plate for a moment, then looked up. She seemed very hesitant. "A month ago I felt . . . a lump in my breast."

I did not stare anymore at Mindy's breasts. I felt bad I had ever stared at her breasts.

"Sarah recommended a doctor. He examined me, sent me for mammograms. Positive."

"Wait a second," I said. Something sounded wrong. "How old are you?"

"Twenty-nine. I'll be thirty this January. Anyway, on the X rays he showed me a lump," she said. "Then he did a biopsy."

I stared.

"It was benign. There wasn't cancer."

"Well, that's great. Great news."

"He scarred my breast."

And very bad news. All surgical procedures have that unfortunate risk.

"There's a two-inch-long scar above my nipple."

Two inches was a large scar.

"He also came on to me," Mindy blurted out.

"What?"

"Came on to me."

"The doctor? Sexually?" I added, which sounded stupid.

"Yes," she said. "Then he hit me."

"Whoa," I said.

"This doctor is bad. A bad person," Mindy said, gripping her butter knife as if she wanted to butter some doctor's face real bad.

"Mindy," I said, "this is stuff for a lawyer."

"I've been to a lawyer. He wouldn't take my case. This doctor's a lawsuit beater."

I knew what that meant. I'm acquainted with lots of long-knife lawyers, and they've told me certain doctors with intimidating libraries of credits and/or acclaimed, powerful friends are pretty much lawsuit-proof. Personal injury lawyers, working on contingency, can't afford to attack the armor of these litigator-proof M.D.'s.

"Who is he?" I said.

"Thomas Brickman. He was in the papers."

A little light went on in my mind. The current administration had offered someone the post of assistant secretary of health. He'd turned it down. Brickman sounded familiar.

"You might have seen him on TV," she added.

I recollected a talk show host chatting with a tall, kindly, white-haired fifty-five-year-old. A bad person who tried to have sex with his patients and then hit them after scarring their breasts? "How can I help?" I asked.

"Your column. That's why I called. Doctors being odds makers? It was in last week."

My column appears biweekly in one of New York's racier tabloids, and the title of last week's was "Doctors: Life's Bookies." It described physicians as risk managers who prescribe aspirin or heart surgery depending on the odds, the odds being risk factors of diseases, patients, and the cures themselves. (My mailbox is already cluttered with angry responses. People want to see their M.D.'s as saints and gurus, not Las Vegas handicappers.)

The point? Performing more procedures than a statistical norm might indicate incompetence or greed.

Doing a statistical survey of Brickman's invasive procedures would be right up my alley. Plus exposing a villain sounded like a fine reason to get involved. "Okay, I think I can help with your lawsuit," I said. "And I know an excellent lawyer. Do you have any other evidence?"

"Evidence?"

"That he's a sloppy surgeon? That he operates at the drop of a hat?" Mindy shook her head.

"That's okay. We'll find some." Though I didn't know how. "How about physical evidence he hit you? Was there a mark?"

She shook her head.

"Were there eyewitnesses?"

She shook her head again. "He has a tattoo," she said. "A serpent and rose."

"A tattoo?"

"On his wrist. It gave me the creeps."

As far as I knew, there was no law against having yourself tattooed with a serpent and a rose.

"I've got this feeling he's evil," Mindy said. "My boyfriend can tell you. Well, not really a boyfriend. His name is Andy Picard . . . a stockbroker . . . lives on the Lower East Side. I can give you a retainer."

"For what?" I said.

"To take my case. To help me get to the bottom of this." And Mindy reached in her coat and held out a little brown paper bag stuffed with . . . "It's three thousand dollars," she said.

Three thousand dollars? I took the bag, pulled it below the table, and watched a roll of hundred dollar bills uncurl like a snake in my lap.

"You can count it," she said.

As the cash did not bite me, I decided to trust Mindy Sayles.

"There's more to tell," she said, "but I can't talk here."

I looked around. Our block of wood was wolfing down his crumbling bacon and unburned toast. Michael was catching a smoke in the back. The place was empty.

"Where do you want to talk?"

Mindy Sayles leaned toward me and whispered, "Your place."

My place? Well, of course, she just wanted someplace private. Down, James. "Okay," I said. "Michael!" I waved my hand for Michael and the check.

Mindy looked over her shoulder, then leaned farther toward me. Six inches away I could smell her coffee breath. "I want to tell you . . ."

"Yes?"

"About a clipping."

A clipping?

"Check!" Michael cried, sliding to a stop beside the booth and delivering the bill like a baton in a relay race. I grasped it in my fingers and looked up at Mindy, who was standing to put on her coat.

I'm not going to describe how great she looked twisting into that. It would be politically incorrect . . . and I might overexcite myself.

"Excuse me." The block of wood held a business envelope in his hand. "She dropped this," he said, placing it in my palm.

I put his envelope in my pocket, then pushed five dollars on the table. Michael always gets a big tip. My life expectancy would plummet if I had to cook for myself.

Mindy waited at the door. I had a beautiful client and lots of hundred-dollar bills. My fantasies of a more exciting life were on the reality track.

"Waiter!' the block of wood cried."Check?"

CHAPTER
3

"Great day!" I shouted as a garbage truck roared past. We were waiting to cross the dangerous stretch of Grove Street, and I touched the thirty one-hundred-dollar bills in my pocket and recalled an adage a black truck driver once told me. Money in your pockets, boy, your hands never get cold.

He meant inner cold. Inner weather. The climate of our security.

Ever wonder why riveters on top of a skyscraper make more than riveters on the ground? Higher risk (literally). Ever wonder why soldiers in Desert Storm got more than their brothers and sisters in the States? Combat pay.

Money and risk go together. The higher the

risk, the bigger the paycheck. I've expressed this several times in my column.

Except nothing seemed risky here. A beautiful sculptor had met me and given me a three-thousand-dollar retainer. The bills in my pocket only brought to mind the joyful phrase *free lunch*.

"New York looks great," I said. Mindy looked around as if this were some kind of revelation, as if she hadn't seen the skyline, the sun, the clouds in months. "Let's cross," I said. We did to the newspaper kiosk. "My office is kind of messy," I added, which sounded totally stupid, like a line I'd heard in a movie or a dream, an adolescent fantasy of trying to get the girl into your apartment. Pubescent déjà vu.

We waited for the light. Though this intersection is dangerous, the odds of getting run over in Manhattan are surprisingly tiny. I was about to share this fact with Mindy when I recalled her mentioning the clipping. "What clipping?" I shouted.

"What?"

"You mentioned a clipping."

"It's something I found in my mom's apartment," she shouted back. "From the *Boston Herald*! Thirty years ago! April!"

"What does this have to do with Thomas Brickman?" I said.

She shrugged.

The light changed. Coming toward us was a Halloween parade. On Sheridan Square it's always Halloween.

"Mr. Denny," Mindy said, "please stay close to me."

"Excuse me?"

"Please stay close. I'm very scared."

"Of course," I said. Scared? "The odds of your getting run over are tiny," I added, hoping to joke her out of her fears. "I think they're as small as one in twenty thousand." She wasn't smiling. I reached in my pocket. "Oh, you dropped this," I said, and took out the envelope. Mindy stared at the envelope as if it were utterly incomprehensible, like a huge radish. "That man said you dropped . . ." I placed it in her hand. She raised it to her eyes. She looked terrified.

Odds setter that I am, I figured the chance of an envelope's terrifying Mindy was pretty small. So I turned to follow her stare. Our Block of Wood stood outside the Apollo.

"What the hell's going on?" I said, turning back to . . . the envelope replaced in my hand.

Mindy was running across Seventh Avenue.

The rest seemed to happen as if in a movie, which is a big cliché, I know, you've heard it a thousand times.

Still, it happened as if in a movie.

A yellow taxi, engine racing, burning rubber, bucked right through the red light and at thirty miles per hour hit her. Mindy ascended into the air, arms and legs akimbo.

Everyone around Sheridan Square froze. It was as if we were all at the circus, a one-ring circus, and on the trampoline, straight from Moscow, was the famous Mindy Sayles. Up, up into the air she flew with the greatest of ease . . . and down she fell onto the trampoline.

An asphalt trampoline.

There was a thud, a loud thud as she bounced. And with that came a collective exhalation of these thirty or so spectators, as if all of them, all at once, had been punched in the stomach.

Someone screamed.

Everything sped up. Tires shrieked, horns blew, people shouted. I ran into the street, slowing before a crowd that had gathered. I pushed through.

And got nauseated in an instant. A minute ago I was next to a beautiful woman, and now I stared at an arm illogically twisted. A eye socket without . . .

I won't continue.

One thing was certain. Mindy Sayles was no longer alive.

Time went by, time accompanied by sun and heat and sounds. And then a siren getting louder.

"You with her?" A hand grabbed my shoulder. I turned, looked up, covered my eyes.

Behind me were other uniforms. EMS boys jumping from an ambulance. Sheridan Square is only five blocks from St. Vincent's Hospital. If you have to get run over, this is one of the better places.

If you live.

"What?" I said. Actually "puffed out" is closer than "said." My voice sounded as if I'd come up for air. Risk-assessing automobile fatalities, something I've done, is not like seeing one in person.

"You okay, buddy?" the cop said. "Hey, Lieutenant, the guy."

"You okay?" said a tall, kindly-looking African-American gentleman in a dark, three-piece suit. "Can you hear me?"

"Yes, oh, yes," I said.

"I'm Detective Grimes. Call me Tony. Can we talk?"

"Yes. Yes," I repeated.

"Hey, get those assholes . . . please excuse my language, Mr. . . ."

"Denny," I muttered. "James Denny." We were beside the kiosk. Someone directed traffic—rather, stopped it. Cars, buses, trucks were re-routed. Sheridan Square was made safe for pedestrians now.

"How are you feeling right now, Mr. Denny?"

"What? Fine. Don't know."

"See what happened, Mr. Denny? Someone said you were with this lady."

"Yes. No. I mean, a cab, I didn't get the number. I didn't . . ." I was making lots of sense.

Lieutenant Grimes passed over a small silver flask, cap open.

"No. No." I pushed it away.

"Would you like a ride to St. Vincent's emergency room?" he kindly asked.

23

"No. No. I'm fine. Shook up. Fine." I think I was now sitting on the curb. I think that's what I was doing, fine as I was.

"Could you try to think about it again and tell me what happened, Mr. Denny?" Lieutenant Grimes quietly continued.

"What happened?" Why was I repeating everything? "She ran into the street."

"Mindy Sayles," Detective Grimes said.

"Yes . . . how'd you know?" I cried out. Lieutenant Grimes stared at me a moment, then produced a wallet with, evidently, Mindy's ID. I looked at her photo. I was thinking about what Mindy said, how the police possibly were following her. . . . I wasn't sure what I was thinking. "She was a client. We were having a business meeting—"

"Where?"

I pointed. Beyond the crowd, up Christopher Street, was the Block of Wood. "Him!" I shouted, jumping up, pointing. "Stop!" But the Block of Wood disappeared.

"Who?" Grimes said, turning without any particular haste.

The man who had frightened Mindy Sayles to death was gone.

"Nobody got the number, Lieutenant," somebody said to Grimes.

"Excuse me," Grimes said.

In the background I heard talk about photographing the tire marks, making sure to search for paint chips on the victim . . . victim. Mindy was a victim. And she had said she was scared of becoming such. She had asked me to stay close, to protect her. And I had managed, well, to tell her how unlikely it was she'd get run over.

"Listen," Lieutenant Grimes said, back at my side, "I'm going to give you my card. We'll send a squad car later to get you, Mr. Denny, for a recorded statement. But if something comes to mind . . ."

"Recorded statement?" I said. I started to recall again what Mindy said about the police.

"This is vehicular homicide, Mr. Denny. Hit-and-run, understand?" I think I nodded. "There any reason . . . does she have enemies, Mindy Sayles?"

"What?" I looked at Lieutenant Grimes. He looked at me.

"Mr. Denny, when you're feeling calmer, we'll talk some more. Put that card in a safe place. That envelope, for instance."

I looked down. In my hand was the small envelope that, if I thought of it, had just cost Mindy Sayles her life. "Right," I said. I stuck the card in the envelope.

"You get home okay."

"Right. Sure."

"Call me if you want, Mr. Denny," Lieutenant Grimes said.

"Right. Sure. Thank you." I managed to stumble away, gripping the envelope like a vise. Across the street on the curb I looked down at it again.

And tore out a piece of paper and read in large hand-blocked letters, WE'RE WATCHING!

I stared at that for about a minute.

A block past the traffic jam Mindy Sayles had created during her last act on earth, I hailed a cab and shouted to the cabbie, "SoHo. Fast as you can!"

CHAPTER
4

What was going on? An hour ago I was doing a census on New England honeybees. Now, after disclosing a secret to me, a person in my presence, who had asked for my protection, had just been killed. And in my possession was evidence, a note with the cryptic message WE'RE WATCHING!

Who were "we"? Watching whom?

Why was I, Dr. Risk, wondering about this?

Down West Broadway above Canal I got out of the cab. I looked around twice to make sure I wasn't being followed. I wasn't sure who'd want to follow me. The Block of Wood? Lieutenant Tony Grimes?

I'd never worried about being followed before. I didn't know how lucky I was.

An hour ago I'd daydreamed about taking risks instead of labeling them. What a mistake. I wanted my risk-free life back.

I quickly made a right on Wooster Street in SoHo, in that cast-iron neighborhood where fiancée and child lived. I raced up three flights of stairs to Sarah's loft.

These cast-iron factories in SoHo got built about 150 years ago, and as elevators then were just a gleam in an inventor's eye, long, straight stairways were built to rise precipitously to the roofs. Freight or whatever slid up or down them. Workers trudged up or down them. About thirty years ago artists trudged up or down them, to use the large spaces as cheap art studios. Then the area got respectable, and now yuppified lawyers and doctors trudge up or down them, having converted the spaces into apartments that would cost even more of a fortune uptown. Sarah luckily got hers from her former husband, a music industry maniac who left her and her child three years ago.

Sarah's loft is as good as it gets. With two thousand square feet and ten windows practically floor to fifteen-foot ceiling, most facing south and yellow sun, it's Southampton in Manhattan. Lest you imagine I just metamorphosed into a slimy real estate broker, I mention this not to sell you the place but to explain why, when I push through the door, I feel transported from my meager basement office of risks and chances into the ample rewards of sunlight, beauty . . . and Sarah.

And right now safety. I didn't think anyone would know I'd go here, anyone being folks intimately involved in writing anonymous letters to poor dead Mindy Sayles.

I reached in a pocket and found a key. Though usually I knock, now I didn't.

"James!" Sarah cried, home for lunch. "Are you all right?"

Why ask that? I wondered until I spotted in a mirror a strange man who had all the blood drained from his face. Possibly a vampire.

"Dr. Risk!" a small child cried: Keri, back from school for lunch. Ah, the sanctity of school, and mothers, and lunches. "You okay, Jamey?" Keri said. Even she noticed.

"Hey, guys, I'm fine," I said in my gruff, macho voice, which was now an octave higher than usual.

There's a Kitchen Area in this loft—a Kitchen Area, a Bedroom Area, a Dining Area—and in the Kitchen Area I sat at the plain oak table on which sunlight shone merrily and placed my head in my hands. I tried to smile and nearly choked.

"Keri, why don't you watch TV?" Sarah asked. Keri nodded sadly and tiptoed off to the TV Area. Six-year-olds know grief doesn't like to be disturbed.

Sarah sat on the chair next to mine. "What happened?" she whispered.

It took a while to speak. "Someone . . . died."

"Oh, my God!"

I stared up. I was too self-absorbed to wonder what Sarah was thinking. "Mindy Sayles," I said.

Sarah stared at me blankly. "Mindy Sayles?"

"Didn't you know her?"

"Oh, yes. Yes! We met and spoke a few times. Oh, that's awful."

I described what happened, how Mindy had called me up, how we'd met, and then the taxi, the sun, the heat, her ascending as if shot from a cannon, which brought back the nausea, the fear, and an instinctive muscular propulsion driving my face now like a homing pigeon toward Sarah's breasts. Women have soft breasts, men strong shoulders, at times nothing sexual about either.

"The cab hit her on purpose," I whispered.

"What?"

"It was hit-and-run. The cab didn't stop."

"Oh, James, hit-and-run isn't on purpose."

That was true. It was leaving the scene that's a crime. Still, I was certain the cab hit her on purpose, and I repeated this.

"How do you know?"

"It's a feeling."

"Oh, James, you're paranoid." Sarah thinks I'm paranoid because I know so many risks. She's partly right. "Did you talk to the police?" she asked. I nodded. "And what did they say?"

"Nothing."

"So why do you assume it was on purpose? James, are you telling me everything?" Sarah said, trying to peer into my skull.

Sarah has sensed my recent restlessness. She's attuned, because she's even more risk-averse than I am. Living seven years with her maniacal, drug-consuming husband radically altered her perspective. She's delighted I'm a risk assessor. Knowing life's risks means avoiding them . . . she thinks.

"All right, it's . . . not just a feeling. I was handed a note."

"What note?" Sarah said, staring.

I pulled the note out of my pocket. "I gave it to Mindy a second before she died."

Sarah looked at the note as if I were holding the tail of a dead rat. "Why is it here?" she cried.

"Sarah, she asked me to get to the bottom of this."

Sarah gaped.

"I promised to help. I'm obligated."

"James Denny, you're obligated to give the police that note!"

"The police are involved."

Sarah stared at me.

"Sarah, it wasn't an accident. Someone killed Mindy Sayles."

"So what? You're withholding evidence! Give the police that note!"

"Okay, but . . . " I reached in my pocket to pull out that other item, the thirty hundred-dollar bills. I threw them on the table. "She hired me."

Sarah looked utterly baffled. She stared at the money, then at me.

She stared back at the money.

Now, I make a very decent income, and Sarah earns a good salary too, but this is New York City, where money quickly disappears, on account of all sorts of things, like rent. Lately Sarah has left lots of hints about an urgent need to feather our nest. The three thousand dollars on the table would buy a bunch of feathers.

"No," she said. "I don't care. Give it back."

"To who?"

"Her family. Charity."

I didn't know if Mindy Sayles had a family. As for charity . . . I gave to charity.

"James, why are you doing this?"

"What?"

"Making me scared. You deal with incinerators. Insurance companies. You figure out risks, you don't take them."

"I'll call the detective, okay?" I said, giving up. "I'll give him the note. Where's the phone?" I stood and almost tumbled to the floor.

"Are you all right?" Sarah cried.

I had to hold on to the chair.

"James, sit down."

"Why?" I asked rhetorically, as I could hardly stand. My legs were rubber. The shock of this morning had caught up in a major way.

"Do you want to lie down?"

"Is it sleepy time for Jamey?" Keri said from the TV Area.

Sleeping was something I felt confident I could do. Anything else I wasn't so certain.

"Come on." Sarah led me by the hand toward the Bedroom Area. "Now, just get under the covers," she said.

"Only if you tuck me in," I said as a joke, but it didn't go over. You see, lately Sarah and I haven't had much fun under the covers. It's the boredom in our lives . . . my boredom.

"I've got to go to work," Sarah said.

"I said 'tuck me,' not—"

Sarah took a swing at me. Tired as I was, I ducked.

I pulled off everything but underwear and crawled in.

Sarah stared at me. "Honey, should I go to work? Are you okay?"

"I'm fine," I whispered.

She sat down beside me on the bed. "I love you, Jamey, you know that. That's why I want you safe and sound."

"Okay."

"Call the police when you feel better, and tell them what you're doing. You will do that, won't you?"

"Roger and out."

"I'll talk to you later," she said, kissing me softly on the forehead, then standing and smiling sadly before leaving the room.

In the background I heard the TV shut off and Keri say, "Is he sick?" All pleasant, familiar sounds. Finally a door closed. Sarah was off to work at an advertising firm not far from here. Keri went back to school.

I sighed, shrugged, and fell asleep.

And I dreamed of a force hurtling toward me. And a voice crying, "Don't resist! Take the risk!"

I opened my eyes and looked around. Boy, had I been resisting. I was resisting the goddamn linen. The sheets and pillow cases and coverlets were tangled around me, clammy with sweat.

Don't resist. Take the risk.

I had been figuring out risks and avoiding them for so long I'd lost any perspective on taking them.

I got up, washed my face, brushed my teeth with my own toothbrush sitting on its own little spot on the bathroom counter, and walked to the Kitchen Area. It was late, almost five. I'd slept three hours and felt punch-drunk. I turned on the small TV and listened to the news. Nothing about Mindy. Hey, this is New York City. To make the *Five O'Clock News,* you've got to kill people, in the plural. Better chop them up too.

I brewed some coffee, looked out the window, and watched the sky over the rooftops turn different shades of pink. I didn't get high on the view. I picked up the phone and dialed my message machine. My messages were hang-ups. I hate that. I got the card given me by Detective Grimes, studied it a moment, stuck it back in my pocket, and dialed information.

"Mindy Sayles?"

I got a number with a TriBeCa exchange and an address. I dialed the number and heard a familiar voice. "Hi, it's Mindy. Leave a message."

I hung up. I dialed again.

"Hi, it's Mindy. Leave a message."

I couldn't believe she was dead. I couldn't believe I was hearing her voice, requesting a message that would never get returned. I wanted it different. I wanted the last five hours to rewind and produce another ending. Don't they do that in Hollywood, preview an ending, and, if John Q. Public hates it, re-shoot?

I wanted to re-shoot.

Unfortunately I could only risk-assess the causes of her way-too-early conclusion. And take the risks that implied.

The scariest risks offer the largest rewards.

So before Keri returned from school and before Sarah came home from work, I carried Sarah's three-speed down three flights of stairs (in rush-hour traffic, biking by Canal Street is the fastest way to go). I set the bike on its wheels, set myself upon the seat, and pedaled toward Mindy Sayles's artist studio a mile away.

CHAPTER
5

It's risky riding a bike. In our country each year one thousand cyclists get fatally struck by four-wheeled predators. The risk per mile? One in two hundred thousand. Meaning if you bike two hundred thousand miles (three-quarters the distance to the moon), you've got a sixty-forty chance of getting crushed by a four-wheeler.

Of course, most of us bike just a mile or two at a time, what I was doing.

But this is New York City, where the sign on the Statue of Liberty should read, GIVE ME YOUR POOR, YOUR HOMELESS, AND I WILL MAGICALLY CREATE HOMICIDAL CAB DRIVERS. One had just murdered poor Mindy Sayles. Others right now were zeroing in on their primary target, the New York City bike rider. Me.

Pedaling just a mile to Mindy Sayles's loft seemed fraught with danger.

I review risks for a practical purpose. Knowing risks shrinks anxiety. Knowledge makes us braver. Risks we understand seem less frightening than those we're in the dark about.

Thus my calculating the odds of getting to TriBeCa in one piece, sneaking into Mindy Sayles's loft, not finding a heavily armed murderer there intent on doing me in, and discovering what she'd discovered and been followed and possibly run over for.

And the odds of succeeding at all this?

Slim.

Mindy Sayles's loft was in one of my favorite spots in the city, in the far corner of TriBeCa near the Hudson River. Old factories and warehouses cluster only a stone's throw from the waterway old Henry sailed up three hundred years ago. Now, three hundred years are a bunch of lifetimes, but on these archaic streets you can still picture tall sails moored on docks and seamen and whalers drinking in pubs.

Plus I even knew the address of the former two-story factory filigreed in red brick; a century ago even factories had aesthetics. I once had a fantasy of buying this building if my own ship, tall sails or not, came in.

The sidewalk was raised as a docking station. I locked the bike onto a cast iron gate across the street and climbed concrete steps to the main entrance. I walked inside.

Something smelled awful.

I slowly climbed the wooden stairway. I had no gun, no knife, no blackjack, so the odds were good that if someone grabbed me, patted me down, and found no weapons, he'd think I was just making a social call. And let me go.

Dr. Risk. Dr. Wishful Thinking.

I turned a corner. The large steel door to Mindy Sayles's loft was open. The odds of lots being wrong soared.

I bit my lip and inched carefully through the doorway. Stopped.

Somebody had been here with a sledge-hammer. And brought along several muscle-bound, hell-bent friends. Faced with what it doesn't expect, the mind plays tricks, and a moment passed before I realized what a thorough search had occurred. In the front of the loft, a living space, Mindy's standing closets no longer stood; they were emptied and upended. Clothing was tossed everywhere. Her bed was torn apart. A file cabinet was turned over; books were tossed from shelves. On a rolltop, a computer was smashed. Everything was smashed. Someone had either found something and destroyed everything or found nothing and destroyed everything.

But what was that smell?

I carefully stepped over clothing and books on my way to a door near the back. They'd done a commendable job soundproofing this building from the continuous din of traffic nearby and thus ensuring privacy for anyone intent on smashing it up. I took out a handkerchief for the doorknob so as not to smudge the prints. This beginning detective knew something.

I pushed the door open. And gagged.

The smell was overwhelming, overpowering. But it wasn't the smell of death and decay.

This was the smell of rotten eggs.

Holding my nose, I looked around. Mindy's sculpting studio was huge, about the size of a baseball infield, with blocks of translucent glass allowing in light, but no view. The ceiling was twenty-five feet high—these lofts are famous for space in every direction—and it framed several large metal sculptures about fifteen feet in height. The sculptures, titled *Rape #109, Rape #204,* and so on, were burnished with a strange brown sheen that at another time might have seemed aesthetically pleasing. But this was not the moment to appreciate art.

On a bulletin board were invitations to a minor gallery opening and a copy of a newspaper review, which I very quickly scanned. Favorable review. Mindy had been on the bottom of a very tall ladder raised toward success.

Near the back of the studio stood an old marble-topped bench and beside it a number of buckets containing, I imagined, pigments and acids. This could have been a medieval alchemist's workbench. Maybe the alchemist was making elephant feces. I now had that handy handkerchief over my face, but it wasn't doing much good. I turned on a faucet—to hell with fingerprints—and wet the linen down before sticking it over my nostrils again.

Whew.

What had happened? The smell of rotten eggs is the smell of hydrogen sulfide. Hydrogen sulfide gets formed by mixing strong acids with any kind of sulfide. Such chemicals get found in laboratories, not artists' studios.

Another thought. Why had the interior decorators, who had so thoroughly rearranged Mindy's living quarters, not laid a heavy finger here?

I'd seen enough. I'd smelled enough. In my pocket was the card Detective Grimes had handed me. Enough Lone Ranger. Time for a phone call.

I heard a click.

I whirled around, like all the detectives I'd ever seen in movies, holding a gun, ready to fire. Except I had Grimes's business card in hand. A business card does not even vaguely look like a gun.

But no one had entered the studio. No one had jumped from behind a door.

The noise had come from an open gas hood built into a wall. Beneath it was a section for welding; an acetylene torch and a welder's mask hung ominously on hooks. As I got closer, the hydrogen sulfide smell got stronger. Boy, did it get stronger. I tried not to gag.

And here it was! Under the gas hood on a concrete drainage floor was a witch's brew, a rigid plastic bucket of black bubbling gook. I knelt to read stenciled writing on the side: BLACK PIGMENT CONTAINING LEAD SULFIDE. I guessed another bucket nearby contained hydrochloric acid. Pour that into lead sulfide and you get rotten eggs.

But you don't get a cuff link. The enamel of one was being eaten by acid spilled on the floor. What were the odds of a cuff link's being on this cement floor under a gas hood?

Rotten, like this stench.

I looked around a bench and found a large piece of this probability puzzle.

Lying on his back, staring me in the face, was the Block of Wood. Only he was no longer digesting his crumbling bacon and medium eggs.

I screamed, backed off, hit my head on something, and toppled over backward. I crawled on the floor toward the door, jumped up, grabbed the knob, and raced out of Mindy Sayles's loft, out of the building, out of my skin.

CHAPTER
6

Forty-five minutes later I was back in the loft. Only I wasn't alone. Kindly accompanying me were Lieutenant Tony Grimes, a police photographer, a criminologist, a technician dusting for fingerprints, two other investigators in plain clothes, and about five others in uniform. We had enough policemen for a Police Athletic League.

One phone call had brought all these nice gentlemen together. I'd made it myself outside on a public phone on Washington Street, rather than on Mindy's cordless (to avoid leaving my prints). I'd had to dial the number three times. Trembling fingers make it really hard to read a business card.

Grimes picked up on the first ring. "Detective Grimes here," he said.

I've no idea what I said, something like "Help, someone's dead, help me!" Something really close to the vest.

After hanging up, I sat on the curb and tried to think. But that part of my brain, the thinking part, froze. So I just stared at the building, at the sunlight, the lovely surroundings, and thought, *Nice day. Nice day.*

There were a couple of cars across the street and a van with a funny-looking license plate—commercial van with no windows. Along Canal Street the tunnel traffic honked. Weary commuters, trying to get home, fumed in their cars, cursing the view. I was reminded of a poem by W. H. Auden: "the torturer's horse/Scratches its innocent behind on a tree." Someone dies, tortured, screaming, but the horse doesn't care. Ten thousand commuters a block away don't care.

Of course I didn't know if our Block of Wood had been tortured, though inhaling ten thousand sick farts all at once couldn't be fun.

Whew. What a way to die.

I wasn't certain hydrogen sulfide did the trick. I did know the Block of Wood was dead. I know what a dead face looks like. I had practice this morning on Sheridan Square.

When was it exactly that risk-free risk assessing flew out the window?

"Fancy seeing you here, Mr. Denny," Lieutenant Tony Grimes now said, shocking me out of recollection. Sitting on a chair inside Mindy's loft, I had turned to watch one investigator, rubber-gloved, carefully pick up a pencil and place it in a plastic Baggie. Beside him a uniformed cop, in a high-tech transformation for the NYPD, typed out a label on one of those automatic labeling machines: "P-e-n-c-i-l."

"What?" I said.

"Fancy seeing you here," Grimes repeated over his shoulder. He was trying to switch on Mindy's home computer. He was having a hard time with that, as the main unit, the hard drive, was smashed like an accordion. "Paying a social visit?" he added.

We hadn't really chatted, Tony and I. We ought to. We'd seen each other enough today to become bosom buddies.

"Social visit?" I muttered.

"Well, Mr. Denny, I expect it is a social visit. You probably just forgot that poor Ms. Mindy Sayles was dead."

Nothing like sarcasm to cement a new relationship. "Uh, Lieutenant," I said, deciding to power right through this and be helpful, "the computer won't work. Hard drive's smashed."

"Hard drive?" Grimes said as if referring to a sixteen-wheeler making it up a steep grade. Grimes, safe to say, was not computer-literate.

"Unless the FBI or National Security has a way of reconstructing those heads, whatever's on them is dead." I knew something about data storage. I'd double-checked the odds of hard drives crashing for a consumer magazine.

"So you're an expert," Grimes said. He dropped the plug and slowly stood.

"A bit," I said.

"A bit? Myself, I never got the chance. Too busy catching the bad guys, know what I mean?"

I stared at Grimes. He stared at me. Were we talking?

"Now, some folks say it doesn't take long to learn about this computer stuff, but that may depend, Mr. Denny, on what you mean by long." Grimes had pulled over a chair that had already been dusted for prints and sat on it, rubbing his dark hands. "Long to me, Mr. Denny, is the time between ordering coffee and putting my sugar in. That's what I mean is long. I don't like to wait, in case you don't know what I mean."

I stared at the man.

"So, what were you doing here, Mr. Denny? I don't think you mentioned . . ."

"Investigating," I said.

"Ah." He stopped rubbing his hands and started scratching his chin. "You're an investigator."

"Well . . ."

"Licensed?"

"Not exactly . . ."

"Because if you were licensed, you should have informed me the first time we said hello. When was that, Mr. Denny? When we said hello."

"Said hello?"

"Late morning, I think. Sheridan Square. Correct me if my memory fails, Mr. Denny."

The odds were good this detective had tried his hand onstage.

"Late morning we meet, and you're pretty shook up, I recall. Now it's late afternoon and you're inside the deceased's loft. You have powers of recovery, Mr. Denny."

"James," I said.

Grimes stared at me. "Answer my question about your powers of recovery . . . James."

"I had a nap."

The investigator and his label-typing cop had stopped what they were doing to observe this burlesque. They seemed a lot more entertained than I was. "Nap?" Grimes said.

I nodded knowingly. "Naps will do that. Revive the spirit."

"Really?" Grimes smiled. "And how do you feel now after your nap?"

"Rested."

I expected applause.

"Okay," Grimes said, "enough's enough. Get down to details. Did you bike here? And walk in and no touch?"

"I touched the sink in the lab. The knob, I think. Lieutenant?" I said.

"Yes?"

"Can we speak privately?"

"James," Grimes said with a kind of sad affection, "we're policemen here. Policemen and doctors have to be told everything."

I looked at the other cops, all suddenly busily back at work. Well, Mindy's fear of police involvement was wildly improbable. A conspiracy involving New York City bureaucracy was by definition an oxymoron.

So I told Grimes most of what Mindy told me, her fears, the mention of a clipping, and her problems with Dr. Brickman.

When I finished, Grimes stared at me. "That it? You're now telling me everything, James?"

"To the best of my recollection."

"To the best of your recollection. If you'd recollected better this morning, that man might not be dead."

As if to emphasize this eerie possibility, an EMS troop came clattering up the stairs, carrying a stretcher. I turned and watched nervously.

"So this guy you called the Block of Wood was at the restaurant?" Grimes asked.

I turned back. "Oh. He gave me this note." Oops. Forgot about the note. I pulled it all crumpled from my pocket.

Grimes did a very professional double-take at that. He stared at me a very long time, then took out a handkerchief and with it pinched the tip of the note carefully. "I'd love to keep this, James, unless that inconveniences you. Even with your fingerprints all over it now. Does that inconvenience you? Or perhaps you planned on dusting for fingerprints yourself?"

The studio door opened, and Arnie Kuzlowski, the medical examiner, dressed in a lab suit with a gas mask around his neck, walked out. He was holding pieces of ID, a wallet, credit cards. Seeing the EMS crew, he said, "All yours."

"What's that smell?" an EMS guy said. Inside they had turned on the gas hood, but it still stank.

"What you got, Arnie?" Grimes asked, turning away from me with a frown.

"Pretty sure he got snuffed by the gas," Arnie said, shaking his head. "Looks like he slipped, got a bump on his head. That floor was slippery. Knocked over those chemicals."

"That's what James suggested," Grimes said.

Arnie looked at me as if for the first time. "You the one who called?"

"James Denny," I said. I looked twice at Arnie's rubber-gloved hand before deciding not to shake it. "Hydrogen sulfide can kill in a couple of minutes. I've done risk assessments on poisons. Were his eyes pink? Pink means hydrogen sulfide."

Arnie stared at me again. Did he have a clue what I was talking about? "Yeah," Arnie said, then turned to Grimes, having obviously seen enough of me. "My guess is he was snooping here, heard something, and was trying to find a place to hide."

"Ah," said Tony Grimes. "Maybe he heard Mr. Denny." He and Arnie turned toward me. They stared a moment.

My mouth dropped. "I'm a suspect because I walked up the stairs?"

Grimes winked at Arnie, who smiled. Oh, joke.

Arnie gave Grimes the pieces of ID, which Grimes stuck in a plastic Baggie. Almost as soon as he'd zipped the bag, the uniformed policeman handed him a label. "ID." Obviously productivity was way up at Homicide.

"Want to go inside, James?" Grimes asked almost cordially after staring after Arnie. "Maybe the smell isn't so bad."

We walked back into the studio to watch the EMS troop zipping up the body bag. They looked kind of green.

I stared down at the body bag. Someone really had hated that smell.

"You're an expert on poisons, James?" Grimes asked.

"I've done studies. Environmental reports, municipal dumps, chemical plants."

"Mmm," Grimes said, kind of noncommittal. "You're also an expert on art?"

We were walking among Mindy's brown metal sculptures. One looked like a large corrugated bug. "No," I said. "You?"

"My son studies that in school."

I turned to Grimes. He looked a few years younger than me. "How old is your son, Lieutenant?"

"Eight." Grimes grinned. Art lover.

We continued on our unguided tour.

I told Grimes that you mixed hydrochloric acid with sodium fluoride to etch metal. That's probably why the acid was here. The lead sulfide was an ingredient in artist paint.

"So these two things get mixed by accident and you get that poison?" Grimes asked.

"That guy could have knocked over that gallon container of acid, splash, into the pigment," I said. "Bam, instant hydrogen sulfide."

"What does the shit do, stink you to death?" Grimes said, shaking his head.

"More or less. The gas paralyzes your breathing."

"I've got a feeling it makes you happy not to breathe," Grimes said, making a face.

"It takes about thirty minutes to kill."

"James, you're a regular encyclopedia."

I was about to say that every municipal dump contains more of this than the folks living next door want to know about; that is why risk assessors are experts on the compound. I didn't.

"So in your opinion it was an accident?" Grimes said after a pause.

"Or somebody wanted it to look like one," I said. "Leaving a container of hydrochloric acid unstopped and on a shelf, ready to fall, seems pretty irresponsible. Mindy must have known the dangers of the chemicals she was using." Then again, our Block of Wood, in snooping, might have unstopped things. "Did you find that clipping Mindy had mentioned to me?" I asked. "*Boston Herald*, 1964?"

Grimes shook his head. He stared at the ID in the plastic Baggie. "Maybe Mr. Washburn found it."

"Mr. Washburn?"

Grimes stared at the ID. "That's your Block of Wood's name. He's getting paid to look."

"Paid?" I said.

Grimes looked at me. "That's right, James, I think you're trying to be in the same business. It says Mr. Washburn was licensed."

"Licensed?" I stared down at the body bag.

"In the state of Delaware," Grimes continued, reading, "Mr. Washburn is a licensed private eye."

CHAPTER
7

When the sun went down, the weather changed, as weather tends to do in New York City, and it started to rain. In the police cruiser the wipers swept back and forth in a hypnotic repetition that sort of harmonized with the splashing tires.

In the backseat Sarah's bike bounced. Grimes was giving it and me a ride back home. Home meant my place. I'd decided that Grimes wasn't going to know a thing about Sarah.

The cruiser's shortwave started squawking. Grimes clicked it off. "Breaking precinct policy," he said with a grin.

I nodded. Whatever Grimes said seemed subject to various interpretations.

For my part, I wasn't sure how to interpret the past six hours.

Dave Washburn, a private eye from the state of Delaware, had sat incognito beside me this morning, ordering breakfast. He'd followed me into the street and later burgled Mindy's loft. A half hour ago he'd got rolled out of it in a body bag. Was his the line of work I had fantasized about pursuing?

Anyway, what did Washburn, a detective from Delaware, have to do with Mindy Sayles, a sculptor from, I imagined, Boston?

"Who said rain?" Grimes grumbled, peering through the murky half-moons the wipers created.

"As an expert on risk, Lieutenant," I said, "I feel duty-bound to tell you that weather numbers are not accurate."

"You're saying the weather's a fib, James?"

"Fib's a strong term, Lieutenant," I said, and grinned. Grimes turned and stared.

I told Grimes I'd done a study for a shipping firm that wanted to sue the National Weather Service. The service had completely missed a storm that sank a ship. It had predicted something like 100 percent chance of sunshine.

All hands lost.

"Lost at sea?" Grimes said, peering through the windshield as if at a weedy aquarium.

At the time I had calculated the service's accuracy for two days to be a coin flip. Fifty-fifty. With precision like that, you could bet on your bunions.

"Win the case?" Grimes said.

"Lieutenant, there are rulings going back to the dawn of time stating that weather is an act of God. You can predict an act of God, but don't bet on it."

I was wondering about predicting how long it would take us to get home. Thanks to the rain, we were mired in traffic.

"You actually do this for a living, figure the odds, shit like that?" Grimes asked.

"Shit like that?" I said, laughing.

"Like my chance of getting hit? I'm serious. You know, line of fire?"

I turned and stared at Grimes. His profession was riskier than most. "They're just odds, Lieutenant. There's no certainty."

"I know that, James. I'd just like to know my chances in case I want to make a bet." And Grimes smiled.

The man had a sense of humor, which he probably needed in his profession. "Well," I said, "the field of risk theory is kind of tricky. You should read my newspaper column."

"Next time I look at the paper, I'll give it a go."

"It's in every other Thursday."

"Yeah. Hey, know what I like to read when I get the time? Detective mysteries."

"Really?" I said. "That's surprising. You'd think they'd pale beside real police work."

"Mysteries don't remind me of real work," Grimes said. "That's why I like them. They take my mind off real work. Mysteries have nice neat endings, crimes solved, bad guys sent downtown, good guys smelling like a rose." Grimes gave me a wistful smile. "I like those kind of stories."

Of course. We all love stories that end with neat solutions. Stories that make sense.

In contrast to real life.

"Sounds like risk theory," I said.

Grimes raised his eyebrows. "Risk theory?"

"Take a fender bender in the rain," I said, trying for some reason to make a point despite the poor chances of success. Grimes didn't seem like a risk theorist in the making. "You can predict the odds of that happening down to the decimal, factoring in all the risks, time of day, kind of car, age of driver, seat belt, smoker—"

"Smoker?" Grimes said.

"Smokers get in more accidents. Probably due to less regard for health. You can figure how it'll all come out."

"Like a detective book," Grimes said.

"Right. But sometimes you get the craziest results. They're not at all what you expected."

"Like the weather?" Grimes asked.

"Or a crime that doesn't get solved. These unexpected results are called deviations."

"Deviations give you crime in the first place," Grimes said, frowning.

Not a trace of irony there.

"Deviations," I tried to explain, "occur most often in the short run. In the short run you get too few fender benders or too many murders. The

odds get skewed, and nothing is certain except un-
certainty."

"Mmm," Grimes mumbled. I was losing him. Or
depressing him. "Short run. I could do without
that," he said.

I looked at the red, yellow, and white lights
smeared on the windshield and wondered about
the odds of our making it past Canal Street before
the millennium. "When's your shift end?" I asked.

"Ended. Double time now," Grimes said, revived, with a smile.

"You live in town?"

"James," Grimes said softly, "I'm supposed to
ask the questions."

I sighed.

"Like this morning. You get a good a look at
who drove that cab?"

I hadn't. It happened so quickly.

"We've got all sorts of descriptions," Grimes
said, "none matching."

"Matching?"

"Siravindu Singh," Grimes said with a pretty
good accent. He turned to me. "Little Indian guy
with a turban and beard. Driver of the hack."

"Did you catch him?"

Grimes shook his head. "He reported it stolen
a half hour after Mindy Sayles got hit. We found the
cab on North Moore Street, front end smashed to
shit, blood on the windshield. So we went to talk to
him. He thought better of that and split."

"You think he did it?"

Grimes shrugged.

"Why'd he report it stolen?" I asked.

"Maybe to beat the charge. Vehicular homicide."

"Then, after reporting it, why did he run?"

"That, James, is the part that doesn't make sense."

Unless the cab really was stolen and Siravindu ran because he was an illegal immigrant and didn't want to go back to Sri Lanka or wherever he came from.

But that was a pretty large deductive leap. Risk theorists are taught, on hearing hoofbeats, to think horses, not zebras. I was thinking giraffes.

"The point is," Grimes said, "nobody described him in that cab. Turban and a beard. You'd need your eyes examined to miss a turban and beard."

"I didn't see it."

"So? What are the odds nobody did? Figure out the odds on that."

They probably weren't high—eyewitnesses are notoriously inaccurate—but I decided to say nothing more. Grimes, staring out the windshield, seemed intent on his own deductions. Perhaps he was mulling over the unpredictability of human behavior. A detective novel with half the pages missing.

We were heading, finally, through the impasse. Horns honked as if we were conquering heroes. We were. We'd made it to the light.

"Lieutenant Grimes," I said, "one thing about risk theory is certain. If the short run doesn't turn out like you expect, just sit back and wait. The short run eventually becomes the long run, and then risk theory works like a charm. In the long run the numbers come out exact."

"Long run?"

"In the long run the fender bender happens down to the decimal. Long run, deviations disappear."

"Like in a mystery book with those neat endings?" Grimes asked.

"That's it."

Grimes nodded with a kind of sly smile. We had pulled to a stop in front of my building. "Well, I like that. That I like. Here." Grimes clicked open the back door, then got out of the car to help me with the bike. The rain had changed to a drizzle. "Lady's bike, huh?" he said, looking. Hey, he was a detective. Nothing escaped him.

"I got it so it wouldn't be stolen," I said. It sounded plausible. "No macho drug addict would want to be seen riding this."

"Well, James," Lieutenant Grimes said, "this is a gay neighborhood, so your risk just went up. Some drug addict drag queen might love to be seen on this lady's bike."

I stared at Lieutenant Grimes. "Pleasure meeting you," I said.

"Yeah. We may see each other again," Grimes

said with a sigh. "Want to hear more about that long run. I like that long run a lot."

Grimes got back in the car. I opened the gate and wheeled the bike toward the basement, then turned in the mist. Lieutenant Grimes and his cruiser were gone.

CHAPTER
8

The next morning the sun again was shining, but I was holed up inside my little office creating a fault tree involving the death of Mindy Sayles.

If I was going to figure out what happened, I'd better use all my risk-assessing tools.

A fault tree is a pretty simple decision-making flowchart used by most risk assessors. Its main innovation is that it starts from the most fearful, dreadful disaster and works backward along all the routes that might possibly get you there. For instance, a meltdown at your friendly nuclear power plant. You start with the mushroom cloud and figure all the ways it could happen. Then you figure how likely or preposterous each route is.

I wrote MINDY KILLED BY CAB in chalk at the very

bottom of my office blackboard. That was the disaster. Now, what could possibly have caused that?

Siravindu Singh?

Beside his name I wrote, WHY?

For some misguided reason, dreaming of his native Kashmir or perhaps last evening's Knicks game, Siravindu slammed on the gas instead of the brakes and mistakenly roared through the red light. Later, realizing the enormity of his mistake and the punishment associated with hit-and-run, he jumped out of the cab and phoned it in stolen. The police came; he got cold feet and split.

Or?

The cab really was stolen, and someone else ran over Mindy Sayles.

Who?

I branched up from SIRAVINDU and wrote, WHO ELSE?

I had, according to Mindy, a primary suspect: Thomas Brickman. Was it Brickman who had followed her?

There was also Dave Washburn, the detective who, of course, hadn't driven the cab but had handed me a note that chased Mindy into its path.

At the bottom of my fault tree above MINDY KILLED BY CAB I wrote THOMAS BRICKMAN RESPONSIBLE. Above that, I wrote WHY?

I needed to sketch out these routes before deciding how likely or preposterous they were.

Route 1. Mindy Sayles's breast is scarred by

Brickman. Afraid she'll sue, Brickman hires Siravindu Singh to run her over.

Preposterous.

Route 2. Mindy Sayles is sexually harassed by Brickman. Afraid she'll sue, Brickman hires . . .

Not as totally preposterous, but still preposterous.

If I added up Route 1 and 2, it was still preposterous.

Route 3. Dave Washburn plots to have Mindy run over. He gives her a note, WE'RE WATCHING!, which scares her into running into the street. He even signals the cab to hit her.

Also preposterous.

Washburn was an investigator. Whom was he investigating? Mindy Sayles? Andy Picard, the stockbroker who was Mindy's sometimes boyfriend? Thomas Brickman, the doctor? Who were the "we" who were watching?

In the middle of the blackboard I wrote "CLIPPING."

I needed more information. Tons more.

I dialed up Nexis on Mad Max through a friend's account. Nexis is a computer service that goes through just about everything in print. I typed in "Dave Washburn." Nothing. I typed in "Mindy Sayles." There was the mention of that sculpture review and nothing more. "Andy Picard." Nothing. "Thomas Brickman."

Lots.

Dr. Thomas Brickman recently received the

Society of Oncologists' Award. Dr. Brickman was honored at the yearly Chapter Dinner of B'nai B'rith. Dr. Brickman was lauded by the League of Women Voters. Dr. Brickman celebrated a gala tenth anniversary of his marriage to his former fashion model wife. Dr. Brickman formed a medical testing company. Dr. Brickman was offered the post of assistant secretary of health.

This did not seem like an M.D. who needed to assassinate possible plaintiffs.

Mindy had given me a retainer to get to the bottom of this. To get to the bottom of things in our country often requires legal advice.

So I visited Buzz Howard.

Ah, wilderness.

I'm talking about the wilds of Commerce Street, which, from Christopher Street, is a quick left on Bleecker and Seventh and half a block west. Daffodils, hyacinth, crocus, and azalea bushes, plus a tangle of ivy, all compete for space under blossoming ginkgos. Sounds like the English countryside on this noxious isle of Manhattan? It is.

I opened a little gate, tinkled a bell, and walked past all that vegetation, all those flowers, up to a half-open door. On it a wooden plaque stated BUZZ HOWARD, ATTORNEY AT LAW.

Buzz Howard is a legend in the Village. A huge man who played semipro football and wrestled professionally, Buzz got wrongly accused of a crime twenty years ago and, on top of that, poorly represented (if the real perpetrator hadn't confessed, Buzz would have done time). Angry as hell and not going to take it anymore, he gave up the physical playing field for the more dangerous rough-and-tumble of legal gymnastics. He went to Harvard Law, made *Law Review,* and enlarged his brain to the size of his biceps.

"How's it hanging, bubba?" I said inside his office.

Buzz looks like a bubba. He tips in at three hundred pounds, much of which crowds a desk already overloaded with yellow pads, balled-up paper, and miniature busts of Beethoven. The clarity of Buzz's world swims between his ears.

"I got a case here," he said, pushing aside a pound of papers with several pounds of forearm and several pounds of groan, "a guy eats apples with pips, eats lots of them and nearly dies. He wants me to sue the Apple Growers Association or something so they'll stick warning labels on their apples. 'Beware of pips.' "

"The glue would probably cause cancer."

"Right. You'd need a warning label for the warning label." Buzz laughed.

"Causes seem to be getting thinner," I said with some affection. You see, Buzz is one of the great all-time liberals. He's represented landmark cases of racial discrimination in New York housing, most pro bono. Aside from a large brain, Buzz Howard has a very large heart.

"I've got a case," I said, "that may make you some money."

"Years ago," Buzz said with sigh, "I wouldn't have cared."

"Years ago you didn't have a close relative at Yale." Buzz's nineteen-year-old, Jake, is premed at Yale, a disappointment; Buzz had hopes for a professional bowler.

"You're right. Have some coffee."

I poured a cup of French roast coffee from Buzz's Krupp, splashed in heavy cream, spooned in rock sugar, and sipped. "Heaven," I said with a sigh, sniffing and enjoying. "Which is where we'll both be six days sooner drinking this."

Buzz looked up with a frown. "Is that your 'risk of the day'?"

I usually bring Buzz a current risk, in lieu of a rose. Both have thorns. "Caffeine's a carcinogen. Induces cancer of the bladder."

"So I'll get cancer six days sooner. Tell me about the case."

I did, relating all that had occurred the day before. It took ten minutes.

When I finished, Buzz stared awhile. I had told it pretty decently, all things considered, so decently, in fact, the recollection brought back the nausea and fear.

"Shot like a cannon, huh?" Buzz said. "You're starting to lead an interesting life."

"That's a Chinese curse, Buzz."

"Two weeks ago you were totally bored."

I've told Buzz lately about my gnawing aversion to risk-free. Buzz insists there are risks aplenty just in settling down and starting a family.

"Okay, tell me," I said, getting down to business. "My dead client wanted to prove malpractice. Can she still sue?"

Buzz flicked balls of paper off his desk. "Can she? James, this is America, Land of Litigation. Dead or alive, it's your plaintiff's right to sue. Now, tell me more."

"The woman had exploratory surgery under unusual circumstances."

"Such as?"

"She was twenty-nine, probably too young for the aggressive treatment she got. Unless there was a major history, the risk factors were small."

"How big was the scar?"

"Two inches. Near her nipple."

"We can sue for emotional distress until death. How long did she have the scar?"

"A few weeks."

"A few weeks?" Buzz looked decidedly unhappy. "How can I sue for just a few weeks of emotional distress?"

"The emotional distress might have killed her," I suggested.

"How?"

"Made her so upset she ran into the street?" That seemed unlikely. "Buzz, I want to sue."

"I know that. But why?"

"To get his records."

"Whose records are we talking about?"

"Dr. Thomas Brickman."

Buzz's face fell. He sighed, and the balls of papers on his desk fluttered. "*The* Thomas Brickman?" he said. "Look." Buzz spun around on his chair like an elephant on one of those huge circus stools, his ponytail fluttering behind him. He searched in a file cabinet for a moment, then pulled up a mimeographed journal. "Association of Trial Lawyers of America. ATLA to us shysters." He waved the journal around like a white flag. "Three huge cases against him. All went to trial. When they go to trial, you're in the shit." He turned the pages, found the article, and peered into its minutiae. "This one after four years. This, seven. Correspondence, pleadings, briefs, affidavits, depositions, expert witness fees, and your hardworking ambulance chaser's out an easy fifty grand."

"How'd Brickman win?"

"Maybe he had a good lawyer." Buzz stared at the journal. "What'd they almost make him, secretary of health?"

"I don't care."

"You don't care?" Buzz stared at me. Then his eyes lit up. "Wait! You had a thing with your client!" He revised that. "You tried to fuck her!"

I stared at Buzz. "What are you talking about?"

"Your client. Mindy Sayles."

"You've lost your mind."

"I'm not accusing you of necromancy. Or even cheating on Sarah. You just tried."

"I didn't try. I met her once in a coffee shop."

Buzz did some more serious staring, the investigative nature of which turned into befuddlement. "So I give up. Why the attachment to a lawsuit?"

"There is no attachment," I said. That was a lie. There was an attachment: to shaking my life out of its rut. Despite the fear and insanity of yesterday, I was determined to follow through on this, wherever it led.

Mindy Sayles had died asking for my help.

"I've got a hunch about Brickman," I said.

"What are you talking about? You deal in odds."

"I think he killed her."

Buzz stared as if I'd just done a backflip over his coffee machine. He picked up his bust of Beethoven and shook his head. "I think Sarah's withholding her slow hand and your brain's full of fudge."

"I'm serious."

"Dr. Kildare after fifty years borrows a taxi and runs over his patient. Why?"

"That's what I need to find out. Listen. The woman, Mindy Sayles, told me the guy was evil. She told me she was being followed. She walks outside and gets killed. Enough coincidences and you've got a certainty."

Buzz's face didn't budge.

"I want his records," I said. "You once told me by filing a lawsuit, you could subpoena someone's records. I want the records of his procedures."

"Why?"

"To find an excess of surgery, a trace of fraud, a motive why Brickman might have killed her."

"You want his records," Buzz said with a sigh, sensing my stubbornness. "Okay. To sue, we'll need her family's consent."

"She has no family."

Buzz stared. "So we make you administrator of the estate. It could be done. Still, it'll take years."

"All I want is the number of patients, the number of biopsies, and the ages of the patients. A computer can spit that out in a minute."

"And his three or four lawyers will fight you tooth and nail for a year."

"It might stir something up."

"Don't count on it."

My plan seemed to have lots of holes.

"All right," Buzz said, "if you're in a hurry, I've got an idea." He picked up the journal again and peered through it. "ATLA has an exchange listing for us plaintiff lawyers. I'll call the guys who sued him, see if they'll send us their stuff."

"Their stuff?"

"What they got from their discovery: interrogatories, copies of surgical procedures with the names whited out, things like that."

"How long will that take?"

"Let me see." He walked through the journal

70

with his fingers. "Okay, I know these guys. I kibbitz and cajole, maybe days."

"Great," I said.

" 'Great' with a big question mark. An expensive question mark." Buzz looked down. He seemed hesitant. "James, I love you like a brother. But we're almost destined to lose . . . and I've promised Ellen that big twenty-fifth . . ."

"Say no more." I pulled out my wallet and laid fifteen of Mindy's Ben Franklins on top of his desk.

"What's this?" he asked.

"A recent inheritance. For your retainer."

"I don't need all this . . ."

"You never know."

Buzz slowly smiled. "All right. Dr. Risk means business."

"You betcha," I said with my best Perry Mason grin. "I'm going to get this guy. Watch me."

Ah, chutzpah.

CHAPTER
9

I ambled back to my office. I got a coffee to go from Hakim across the street, unlocked my double locks, and again stared at my blossoming fault tree. It had a big question WHY? atop Thomas Brickman.

What string of activities did Brickman have to perform to kill Mindy Sayles? Hire Siravindu Singh to follow Mindy to the Apollo, wait, and, when Mindy ran across Seventh, do his dirty work.

But what was Brickman's motive? Why would a successful, big shot doctor take the chance of destroying his own life, as well as someone else's?

More information. Risk assessing means gathering information. And the one person I needed to gather lots of information about was Thomas Brickman.

Well, why not meet the man? Why not make an appointment?

Brickman's office phone rang twice before a woman answered. "Julie here," the woman said with a starchy British accent. "Office manager, if you please."

Successful doctors today hire a staff of ten with consulting rooms, nurses, bookkeepers, and an "office manager" to choreograph the mess. "I'd like to schedule an appointment for a breast exam," I said.

"For your wife?" replied the nattily clipped Brit accent.

I had a brainstorm. "Uh, me. Myself," I said.

Silence on the office manager's end of the line.

"I feel a lump. Under my nipple," I said. "I'm very worried."

More silence. Finally, hoarsely: "Very good, sir."

"My uncle died of breast cancer," I added. That, God help me, was actually true.

A computer keyboard clicked in the background. Julie said that usually there was a two-week wait to see the doctor, but as I was worried, and as she'd just gotten a cancellation, would 3:00 P.M. be satisfactory? I replied, "Pip-pip, jolly good."

I had called Lieutenant Tony Grimes yesterday afternoon to find out if he'd made any progress. Oddly enough, Tony was noncommittal. No, they hadn't found the cabdriver. They hadn't found any family for Mindy Sayles. He didn't want to hear any more about my theories. There was no need to call again about the case.

That wasn't very friendly.

To stanch my disappointment, I surveyed my computer calendar for future projects.

Several new ones demanded immediate attention. An advertising company wanted to know the average number of bubbles in a glass of a competitor's champagne. A maker of bungee-jumping equipment wanted an accurate assessment of the dangers of the sport (I'd make sure to get paid in advance for that). A man in Philly would pay me a thousand dollars just to advise him on the true odds inside Atlantic City's casinos.

In short, there were thousands of dollars of work staring me in the face if I'd just pick up the phone and walk with my fingers.

I decided to walk with my feet. I stood and got my coat.

I got on Sarah's ancient three-speed again to go crosstown—crosstown is much safer than riding on avenues—and there I locked it on a meter and took the Lexington Avenue subway up to Eighty-sixth Street.

Now biking and taking the subway may seem bush league for a fairly well-to-do risk theorist, but the savings in time and money, plus the exercise, easily beat raising your hand and hailing a cab. I'm not cheap, just efficient. And efficiency, we've noted, diminishes risk.

Exiting at Eighty-sixth, I walked a block to Park. Brickman's office was past a main entrance behind a black iron gate. I pressed a buzzer and entered.

Light flooded through southern windows. Sprinkles of pansies sprouted from vases. The walls were eggshell white. I had an urge to meet the interior decorator instead of the good doctor.

Good doctor, my foot.

I took the customary forms from two pretty, smiling nurses—the Brit office manager was nowhere in sight—filled them out, handed them in, and went back to my seat. I perused the cartoons of two months of *New Yorker*s, the football season of *Sports Illustrated*, and two continents in *National Geographic*. I was about to take out subscriptions to all three when one of the pretty nurses walked up to me and whispered, "The doctor will see you now."

She led me down a hallway just a little too short for a street, past ten waiting rooms. Ten. I counted.

"You can take off your shirt," the nurse said as we entered a room.

"You first," I replied inspirationally. I got a very unhappy look about that . . . and a slammed door. I guess I could scuttle my wisecracks.

Waiting for Thomas Brickman, I looked around. There was a white cabinet with sutures and gauze and another cabinet drawer with rubber gloves and vials, all the usual examining room stuff. What had I expected to find? Bloodstains? A confession of sins?

The door opened, and Dr. Thomas Brickman walked in.

Let me record my impressions. First impressions, I've found, are usually more accurate than seconds and thirds.

Approaching me was a cultured, kindly, sensitive old-world physician with a full mane of silvery hair and Mediterranean blue eyes. His large nose was Romanesque, his eyebrows were dark and bushy, and the rest of him was deeply tanned, indicating a winter spent avoiding northern climes. He was tall, over six feet two, with the lips of an intellectual and the blue-veined fingers of, well, a skilled surgeon.

In short, the man was a prototype. I almost immediately started to disrobe.

Except there was a spoiler, the tattoo on his wrist, the one Mindy Sayles had described, of a serpent and a rose. It definitely didn't belong there, that tattoo.

I'd read a study on tattoos. Tattoos and crime, it seem, go hand in glove. Criminals like tattoos, and though that hardly seemed proof of Brickman's culpability, it added to the chances. Very slightly.

"What seems to be the problem, young man?" Brickman said. I looked up from the serpent and rose at a man fifteen years my senior. "Young man" is a relative term.

"I'm not sure," I said, suddenly very nervous.

Brickman glanced at his chart. "Let's see. Swelling beneath the right nipple? May I see?"

The idea of faking a lump in front of the famous doctor grew less alluring by the second. Brickman was an expert in his field. I was an amateur in mine.

Brickman folded his arms around the chart. "Mr. Denny," he said with a big sigh, "please relax. I understand men have trouble talking about their fears."

Men have trouble talking about the fear of being found out as frauds. "Men rarely get breast cancer," I offered.

"You have a history. Take off your shirt. Take off your shirt, sir."

Reluctantly I did.

Brickman made me sit on one of those tables with the white butcher paper you noisily scrunch up. He pointed a hot lamp directly at my breast. "Of course, we can't do a regular mammogram for this tiny a subject," he said, suddenly squeezing the tiny subject, my poor naked nipple, as hard as he could. He looked up. "Did you feel something?"

"Yes, yes!" I cried. My nipple was throbbing.

"I mean right behind the nipple. Here," he said, squeezing hard again.

"No!" I shouted, trying to get my backside, levitated by the pain, back down on the butcher paper. I nearly pushed him away.

"Mr. Denny, I felt something."

"I understand," I said, panting and nodding vigorously to make that absolutely clear.

"Well, I can suggest a fine-needle aspiration biopsy." He stared into the mysteries of that chart, then placed two fingers together in a pincer. "We insert a very thin needle into the area to draw out cells."

A long needle touché into my nipple? "No, I don't think so. Really."

"Mr. Denny, the risk of male breast cancer with a history isn't entirely insignificant."

"The risk of male breast cancer," I said quickly to get out of this, "is only, over a lifetime, one percent. A thousand cases per year. I've got a better chance of getting killed by a falling object."

Brickman looked at me with a kind of bemused suspicion, then stared back at the chart, as if he'd missed on it a history of growing antlers. "How did you know the risk of male breast cancer is one percent?"

"I'm a risk assessor."

The machinery clanked behind Brickman's eyes.

"I've written articles," I said, and told him my pseudonym.

"Dr. Risk?" Brickman's eyes aligned like a slot machine. "Yes. Yes! I read you off and on. You look like your photo."

The wrong approach to win my heart.

"I've enjoyed your columns. Except for a recent one. 'Doctors, Life's Bookies?' That's an overstatement, don't you think?"

My mind was elsewhere, thinking of how to draw information from my primary suspect. He had aggressively prescribed an invasive procedure for me. Though not proof of anything, it hinted at a propensity for rash diagnosis.

Doctors, as I said, make decisions based on trade-offs. Good for the heart, bad for the spleen, helps the liver . . .

They also make decisions based on the risks to themselves. Good for the doctor, bad for the plaintiff and lawyer's bank accounts. In short, to protect themselves against the risks of malpractice suits, doctors practice "defensive medicine." They rashly diagnose and overprescribe.

If that was the problem here, nothing could be done. Insurance companies and courts of law, where doctors get sued, favor this overprotective approach. But some doctors overdiagnose for other reasons, like paying off gambling debts or buying their mistress expensive toys.

Investigate, James.

"Do you ever gamble, Doctor?"

"Excuse me," Brickman said.

"Junkets to Atlantic City, blackjack, things like that?"

Brickman stared at me, amazed. "Mr. Denny, I've never gambled in my life."

This direct approach was decidedly more scientific than psychological. "Doctors like the fast lane," I said. "Wine, *women*, and song?"

Brickman glanced again at the chart, perhaps to consider a referral to a psychiatrist. "Mr. Denny, I've been happily married for the last ten years."

What could I hope to discover: that the doctor didn't wash his hands?

The only approach left was to stir the pot and see what bubbled to the surface. So, bare-chested, I courageously and straightforwardly told Brickman I was here on account of Mindy Sayles.

It was certainly a good thing he'd tweaked my nipple before. His blue eyes shrank to slits, his lips tensed into a jagged scar, and I suddenly had a picture of Brickman holding a scalpel, but not to heal. "You accused me!" he cried.

"What?"

"Yesterday! Some detective came and asked questions. A witness accused me." Brickman was throwing a very inappropriate fit. "You!"

What was he talking about? I told him I hadn't accused anyone. Mindy Sayles had told me what I'd related to the detective.

"She accused me! She's a liar! A notorious liar! And why are you here?" Brickman added.

"Mindy Sayles is my client. She's filing a lawsuit against you."

"I knew it, I knew it!"

"Knew what?"

"You've met me under false pretenses!"

"I contacted you because of a lump," I said, "which you felt, if I'm not incorrect."

Lots of circuits exploded behind Brickman's eyeballs. He had become, after all, my doctor. "Fine," he said with a snarl. "Keep an eye on that nipple."

An eye on my nipple?

"And now please leave."

"Aren't you curious why she's suing?" I asked. "She said you hit her."

"What?"

"She told me," I repeated, "you hit her." Did Brickman think I meant run her over?

"That's another lie!"

"She told me you came on to her sexually."

"This is outrageous!" he cried. "I want you to leave this instant."

"All right," I said, "all right."

But Brickman was already gone, the door slamming behind him.

I put my shirt on, buttoned up, and walked down the hallway.

Whew. That was unpleasant. Brickman had a temper as explosive as Mount St. Helens.

Violent anger often springs from fear. Why did a dead person scare this famous doctor?

I walked down the hallway. One thing was certain: Something had spooked him.

One other certainty. Whether Brickman was rashly diagnosing or not, he was making tons of

money. This was emphasized to me by the nurse at the reception counter, the one I'd suggested mutually disrobing to, who handed me a computer printout. It stated I owed Brickman $190 for a breast exam and consultation. Ten dollars a minute to get my nipple pinched! A dominatrix would have been cheaper!

I walked out into the chill. Did my health plan cover "investigating the suspect?"

CHAPTER
10

Thomas Brickman had more credentials than Al-bert Schweitzer. Plus a medical operation on the surface as kosher as Hebrew National hot dogs.

So what next?

Mindy had mentioned a stockbroker and sometimes boyfriend named Andy Picard, who lived on the Lower East Side and had spoken to Brickman. I'd already told Grimes about him and assumed Grimes would inform him of Mindy's death.

Perhaps Picard could tell me more.

What exactly would he reveal? I wasn't sure. When you go about assessing risk, you gather in-formation and hope for patterns, clues, a bigger picture. Private detecting seemed exactly the same.

To discover where Andy Picard lived, I used a simple risk theory axiom. I went for the obvious.

If you roll a pair of dice lots of times, you'll get more sevens than twos. If you scan a paragraph, the letter *e*, not *z*, will probably appear most often.

The highly probable choice is usually the right one.

The highly probable choice among the many ways to find Andy Picard's address and phone number was to look in the NYNEX phone book under "P."

And there it was. Andy Picard lived on Eighth Street amid that alphabet soup of avenues where Manhattan bulges with a comely downtown girth known as the East Village.

I dialed. A man picked up on the first ring and said, "This is Andy Picard."

"Are you a stockbroker?"

"Yeah."

"What's your apartment number?"

"Two D. Hey, who is this?"

I hung up. No sense clogging the phone lines or wondering, straightforward risk assessor that I am, what to ask next. I'd get more information face-to-face.

I called Detective Grimes again. Yes, he hadn't seemed too happy when I asked before about the case. Still, if I was going to act like a private eye, I should keep my police buddy informed.

"Lieutenant Lowery here," someone said over the receiver.

"Is Lieutenant Grimes in?"

"Grimes? Nah. Out."

"Might I leave a message?"

"Shoot."

"I'm going to go check on Andy Picard."

"Hey, who is this?"

"I'm . . . Dr. Risk."

"Okay. Let me write this down."

I waited a minute for him to get a pencil. The NYPD should have a few of those lying around.

I got disconnected.

Somebody else wanted to use the phone. Fine. I climbed back on Sarah's bike, which I had locked up on a Fourteenth Street parking meter when I went to Brickman's, and pedaled toward the East River.

When archaeologists do digs, they often see life in layers. Well, biking toward the East River is like an archaeological dig. Between Third and Second Avenues are sturdy million-dollar brownstones, located in what I might call the Restoration-Gentrification Era. First Avenue to Avenue A is the Slavic-Bohemian Millennium with its Polish bars populated by punk rockers and leather freaks. Avenue B through D is the Hispanic-Desperado Age, where graffiti grow like creeping fungi, reaching heights of ten feet, and buildings exhibit cavelike, gutted aspects, and empty lots have the feel of Mexican fishing villages, all only a mile from the Empire State Building.

This primitive world is not very safe, especially at night, and at six, which is what my watch said, the sun was setting. Six, however, is not eight, which in New York City is prime time for getting shot. After eight your odds of catching a bullet in the Big Apple double.

My business with Andy, if any, would be over by then.

The address on Eighth Street was a six-story building with a large sign reading AFFORDABLE HOUSING, MAYOR DAVID N. DINKINS. Affordable? The building was gutted. Dumpsters surrounded it, though no one seemed in a hurry to renovate. The street was as quiet as a country road.

No, I wasn't going to be long, I nervously repeated to myself as I locked Sarah's three-speed onto a parking sign. In fact, my projected stay diminished further as I pushed open the abandoned building door and heard sound effects from a recent Dracula movie.

Down a debris-littered hallway a rat scurried. Odds were good it was a rat.

I thought of a stockbroker living in this crumbling structure. I thought of Mindy Sayles visiting him. I thought of myself, mild-mannered risk theorist, snooping here. What was wrong with these pictures?

Andy had said No. 2D. Before deciding I'd

made a monumental mistake, I climbed the crumbling stairway.

No. 2D was spraypainted on a large, metal door above a straw doormat, cozy as could be. I knocked three times. My palm was sweating. Other parts of me sweat too, and it wasn't from a hot flash.

"Who is it?" someone growled behind the door.

"James Denny."

"Who the fuck are you?"

Not the friendliest greeting. "I called before," I said.

There was a discussion. The door opened an inch. I saw an eyeball. The door opened more, and a short, dark, handsome man in his early thirties appeared. His long, straight hair fell across his forehead like a claw. His brown eyes registered lots of hostility.

"Andy Picard, I presume?" I said brightly.

"What the fuck's with 'presume'?"

"We've never met," I quickly explained.

"So why are we meeting now, shit-for-brains?"

"Denny, James," I said correcting him with a cough, and mechanically extending my hand.

Over Andy's shoulder I spotted two very large males, one wearing a T-shirt stating in boldface "Shit Happens." Ah, Dr. Risk, you dodo bird, why are you here? "Can I ask some questions?" I hesitantly suggested. "You see, I'm representing Mindy Sayles. My client."

"Get the fuck out of here," Andy Picard said.

Playing hard to get? Fine with me. I turned to go.

"Wait a minute. You said Mindy Sayles? Where is she?"

I turned and stared at Andy Picard. He didn't know?

A phone rang, leading my eyes into the enormous apartment. The adjoining flats had been knocked clear to create a living space covering the entire floor. There were large rugs and modular couches and track lighting and new windows overlooking an empty lot in springtime bloom, all adding up to the kind of space and view that rents for thousands uptown. I guessed Andy's rent was a box of poison for the rats.

"She had an accident," I said. "She was run over, by a cab. She—"

Andy interrupted. "So that's where she was." He turned to his friends. "You hear? Mindy got run over. Crossed against the green." And Andy laughed.

"She's dead," I said.

Andy stopped laughing. He turned back slowly. He stared at me, the sneer gone. He seemed stunned.

"I'm sorry I had to tell you," I said.

Andy said nothing. Apparently he wasn't a complete asshole.

"This must be a shock," I added.

Though Andy Picard seemed concerned, even troubled, he didn't seem grief-stricken.

"I know it's a bad time," I continued.

"Yeah," Andy finally said. "Yeah."

"Still, I'm wondering if I could ask some questions."

"Now?"

"Yes."

Andy stared a second, then slowly nodded.

"You're a stockbroker. Mindy mentioned a firm . . . " She hadn't, but let's see if he'd supply it.

Andy seemed to think for a moment. "Pesky and Rashowitz," he finally said. "You wouldn't know them, penny stocks." He looked over my shoulder.

"You knew Thomas Brickman? Mindy had a procedure at his office. She said you spoke to him," I said.

"What?" He turned back to me. "Oh. I tried to convince him of an out-of-court settlement."

"What did he say to that?"

"Hung up."

"What kind of person did you sense he was?"

"An asshole, all right? Listen, you got to go now—"

"Mindy is suing him."

That got Andy's attention again. "Suing him? Who gets the money?"

I hadn't even thought of money. Money wasn't the point. "Mindy's estate," I said.

"What do you mean? She owes me. I helped out, you know?"

"I'll keep that in mind."

There was noise on the stairs. Voices.

"They're here, boss," Shit Happens said.

"Hey, Picard, who else is with you? No one's supposed to be with you," the voices shouted.

I quickly looked around. I suddenly had this terrible feeling I was in the very wrong place at the very wrong time.

"Man, you're fucking me up now," Andy said in a whisper full of sadness.

"Sorry about that. I'll just leave," I whispered back.

"You can't."

"What do you mean?"

"I mean, you can't," Andy repeated, and emphasized this by grabbing me by my shirt collar and dragging me back into the apartment.

There's an expression, "between a rock and a hard place." It usually nips at the heels of another popular phrase, "when the shit hits the fan." Right now I stood in a very tight spot, covered with crap.

So I acted.

I mentioned that I practice tai chi. I'm not Bruce Lee in sheep's clothing. I simply go to class once a week to study with my little Taoist master, P. K. Chan. I've done so for nine years. I've never used the ancient martial art based on an absence

92

of tension and resistance. Never had to, risk-averse soul that I am.

But I was going to use it big time, you see, because Andy was grabbing and pulling me, and encountering no resistance, he got me flying, crash-bang, shoulder first into his chest. "Oomph!" he moaned, and flew over his rugs and modular couch, tumbling into the picture tube of his giant Sony, which suddenly exploded like a Disney extravaganza, all fire and smoke. Andy was so amazed he fell into a coma.

I heard lots of "shit" 's outside the door, mingled with lots of stomping and running, sounds I'd hoped to hear, as my plan, concocted in about a millisecond, was to follow the confusion out the door and down the stairs.

Except Bluto was in my face, spitting "motherfucker." I blinked to get the spittle from my eyes and felt his paws around my throat. He wasn't measuring me for a shirt size.

When someone chokes you, P. K. Chan says, get his attention. Blow a whistle, spell out SOS, or, as I did now, push your knuckle into a collarbone. Hard. "Hey!" Bluto cried out, looking down at his collarbone and completely forgetting about his plan to choke me to death.

I knocked his hands off, turned—and got a fist in my face. Stars circled my eyes. My tai chi skills, I thought, might need a little work, a few more Sundays' practice, which might be impossible as Bluto had his fat elbow under my chin and was lifting me off the ground entirely by my Adam's apple.

The rest just disappeared.

A guy shone a light in my eye. Something was stuck under my nose, and my sinuses hit the roof.

"You okay? How many fingers?"

"He was out, you know?"

I took this in calmly. I hadn't a clue.

I couldn't remember why I was here or what I was doing. I couldn't even remember the flashes of pain shooting through my skull in thirty second intervals.

"I want my lawyer!"

That was a familiar voice, to go with this unfamiliar headache.

"Hey, Andy, your lawyer just got deported."

The room slowly evolved to vagueness. Andy was in a chair, handcuffed, I think, his two bodyguards on the floor catty-cornered around him, also cuffed. Walkie-talkies squawked. Cops were everywhere.

"The posse came and rescued your ass," someone hissed in my ear. Another familiar voice. Lieutenant Grimes? I extended my hand and got grabbed and pulled. "You almost got yourself killed," Grimes hissed when I sat on another modular.

Killed? News to me.

You see, a very strange thing happens when you lose consciousness from a concussion or even a choke hold. You don't just forget the time you were out. You forget before and after too.

To fill me in, Grimes described my miraculous survival.

An apparent drug deal, apparent because Narcotics had set it up, was about to get busted. The guys coming up the stairs? Undercover. The deal? Made by Andy.

"Andy? What do you mean?" I managed to gasp. "Andy's a stockbroker,"

"That's just one of his sidelines," Grimes said with a grimace. "His main profession is moving cocaine. We've been after him awhile."

"Hey, Lieutenant, look at this!" an undercover cop cried from across the room, holding up a plastic Baggie filled with white powder.

"Those dog heads kept a stash here," Grimes said, amazed. He stared at me with concern. "How's your jaw?"

Jaw? I touched a bandage. "Ouch," I said.

"Pain means you're alive," Grimes said. "You're a lucky man."

Lucky. I guessed I was.

"Someone said you tossed Andy clean across the room. We've got it on tape, in case you want to show your grandchildren," Grimes said with a chuckle. The chuckle disappeared. "James?"

I moaned in response.

"Why the hell did you bike up here like Mary

Poppins and crash my party?" He was no longer smiling.

I told Grimes a little about my visit and conversation with Brickman. I remembered that.

"You what? You talked to what? Why the fuck did you do that, James?" Grimes cried.

"I've got a client," I said. The flashes of pain in my head were now a predictable constant. My throat felt like sandpaper. Even my nipple hurt.

"Client?" Grimes asked.

"Mindy Sayles."

"Mindy Sayles?"

"I'm suing for her estate."

"Your client's Mindy Sayles?"

I thought I was speaking English. I started to nod. Nodding was hard.

"You should have told me," Grimes said.

"Why?"

"Your client's involved with this shit."

"Come on," I mumbled.

"No 'come on,' James. The woman carried. We got a videotape."

I tried to think for a second. Mindy acting as a mule for Andy Picard? Well, it would explain her paranoia about phoning the cops. It would also explain the coincidence of all these people so ungraciously coming together.

"She give you a retainer?" Grimes asked.

I had two of Mindy's hundreds in my pocket.

"It's probably tainted," Grimes said. "We're following the bills."

I couldn't believe Mindy was a part of this. I couldn't believe I had drug money in my pocket. I couldn't believe . . . "Lieutenant, this . . . doesn't make sense."

Grimes shook his head. "Quit thinking, James. It'll make your head hurt more. Can you get home? We'll take you to the hospital if you like."

This was the second time in several days Grimes had offered to take me to the hospital. He was more involved with my health than my internist. "I'm all right," I said, and started to stand. Nope. Back I sat.

Grimes got up and talked to someone. A wave of nausea swept over me. I held it back.

"You going to teach me that blackjack counting stuff?" I looked up. Grimes had returned with a cup of coffee. He held it out. "I talked to friends. They say it works."

I took the cup. It was hot. Was this Andy's Mr. Coffee? "What'd you say?"

"Counting cards is risk theory. I want to learn," Grimes said.

I took a deep breath. It was like early morning. Wake up and smell the coffee.

"You get a free trip to Atlantic City. I drive, my treat."

I seemed to remember someone wanting to pay me a thousand dollars just to talk about that. "Okay," I said.

"Be careful getting home. I've got to go talk to these jerks. You all right?"

I think I said yes.

"Take care of yourself. You're going to teach me card-counting blackjack to win."

Blackjack? I couldn't count the fingers I had.

I was able to get to the door to pay my respects to Andy and friends. "Fuck you," they replied in unison to my kindness.

I tried to nod at them all cuffed together. Nodding was hard.

Grinning was a snap.

CHAPTER
11

On the street I called my answering machine. There was a message from Sarah. I stuck in another quarter.

"James, where are you?"

I looked around. A street sign said Tompkins Square. Arc lights shone; people trudged home from work. "In the street," I said. I think I was certain of that.

"It's seven-thirty. You were supposed to come for dinner."

Well, I couldn't remember everything. Right now I couldn't remember anything. "You finish?" I said.

"No. And Keri's complaining. She wants to eat with us."

"Right there," I mumbled.

I hoisted myself onto the pedals of Sarah's bike—I'd walked it here—and started pedaling through the glitter of the springtime evening in a very low gear. Biking in anything higher would be a death wish.

I had started taking risks to push myself gently toward a more exciting life, not to slingshot myself toward danger at the speed of light.

Somehow I made it to Sarah's in one wounded piece.

"Dr. Risk!" Keri cried, running up to me as I came through the door.

I felt a little better, all that allegedly fresh New York air. "Keriwinkle," I whispered, hoisting her up and spinning her around. Oops. My head.

"James, where were you?"

"Mommy mad?" I whispered to the little banshee above me.

Mommy stood hesitantly a few feet away wearing tight jeans, a big flowery blouse, and looking terrific. I gave her a peck on the cheek. Keri kicked my face. "Ow," I cried.

"Mushy," Keri groaned.

"I'll make you mushy. You hurt me." I angrily set her on the ground.

"James, what's that? Your chin?"

Chin? I touched the bandage.

"James, how in the world did that happen?"

"My chin?" Think, James. "I cut it shaving."

"With what, a jackhammer? The whole area's puffy."

It looked that bad? I hadn't even looked in a mirror. "Actually," I said, "I . . . fell off your bike."

"My God, are you all right?"

"You got a boo-boo," Keri said, reaching to touch my face.

"You should go to a doctor," Sarah said.

I didn't tell Sarah I'd been to a doctor.

"Mommy, can we eat?"

We walked to the Dining Area. At the table I noticed, to my intense discomfort, that I was seeing double.

"What'd Dr. Risk do today?" Keri asked.

"Found the original Jack the Ripper," I said, trying, like a camera range finder, to get two spinach salad bowls into one. "Caught the Brink's robbers."

"Is the bike all right?" Sarah asked.

"What bike? Oh. Yes."

"Are you all right?"

I think she was upset I was just picking at a perfectly done tuna with yellow sauce. Sarah is a wonderful cook, but I was discovering that getting belted in the face plus nearly choked to death can completely kill an appetite.

We retired to the Television Viewing Area. Sarah set one of those small tin espresso makers on the coffee table. I took slow sips while an FM station played Carmen McRae.

"We need a fireplace," Sarah said, staring at the blank TV screen. To my blurred vision it wasn't so blank. She leaned over to give me a kiss.

"None of that," Keri shouted, cycling behind us.

Sarah frowned at her daughter. "Do you think that's a phase, being antiromantic?"

"Wait'll she puts on lipstick," I said. "You'll be riding your two-wheeler."

Sarah laughed. Amazing how I could come up with one-liners while my head spun like a yo-yo.

Sarah leaned against me. "You know, James, I can't stop thinking about Mindy. Did you see the news?"

I shook my head. That hurt.

"It was in the back of the *Times*. Just a few lines. Are you going to return that money?"

"I'm helping Buzz file a lawsuit. It's a retainer." Paid with tainted drug money, I didn't add.

"James, I don't want you involved with that."

"What?"

"Mindy Sayles and this lawsuit."

"Why?"

"It sounds dangerous."

"It's just a lawsuit," I said, my nose growing longer.

"You saw a woman killed."

I saw a whole lot more. Felt a whole lot more. The secret life of Dr. Risk.

We sat quietly. At least Sarah did. My head thumped like a bass drum. "James," she said.

"Yes?"

"You seem preoccupied."

Preoccupied with keeping my eyes from crossing. "Really?"

She laughed throatily. "Yes! But full of purpose. Makes you sexy."

I turned and tried to stare steadily at Sarah. Had she said "sexy"?

"Oooo, Mommy said the S word!" Keri cried.

"Keri!" Sarah cried, sitting up and glaring. "That's enough. Time for bed."

The phone rang on the coffee table as Keri biked away. Sarah looked torn about chasing her. "Calling Dr. Risk. Dr. Risk," we heard on the answering machine. Sarah clicked on the speaker.

"Buzz Howard," she said, annoyed, "this is not his office."

"Ah, the beautiful Sarah." Buzz's voice scratched out. " 'She walks in darkness—' "

"You're going to walk in darkness, buster. I'll sue you for coitus interruptus." She winked at me. I arched my eyebrows. Coitus interruptus?

"Whose coitus was interrupted?" Buzz asked.

"Hang on, Buzz, I'll get it in the other room," I said.

"Your good friend Dr. Risk's!" Sarah cried. "I'll try to revive him."

This line of humor was (1) highly unusual, considering our recent sexual history, but (2) not very funny, not to me. There'd be no coitus interruptus involving this risk theorist tonight. I was unsure if any of my body parts worked, let alone that one.

I walked to the Kitchen Area and picked up the phone.

"She was kidding," I said.

"Too bad," Buzz said, "for you."

"Buzz, I've had a very interesting day, which I'll tell you about. I need wrestling tips." The windows in the kitchen seemed to pulse back and forth. I needed neurological tips.

"Well, I've got information on Brickman," Buzz said. "Want to hear?"

"Sure."

"His medical testing company is going public."

"What medical testing company? Oh, that one."

"Hey, you okay?"

"Yeah, sure. What do you mean, public?"

"An offering next week on the NASDAQ. He stands to make a fortune."

"What's the name of the company?" I asked.

"Healers Inc. They've got a new AIDS self-test. Requires a urine sample, takes twenty seconds, and is ninety-seven-point-eight percent accurate."

"An AIDS self-test?"

"FDA approval is a lock."

"How's it sold?" I managed to ask. "By prescription?"

"Over the counter, like a pregnancy test. They'll sell millions. I have the prospectus, in case you want a look."

"You going to be long, James?" Sarah cried from the Sleeping Area.

"I'll get it tomorrow," I said to Buzz on the phone. "I've got to go. Duty calls."

"Time to prime the pump?"

I stared at the receiver. It didn't appear to expand and contract. "Buzz, at this moment my pump is broke and the well is dry," I said. And I hung up.

I walked into Sarah's Sleeping Area. "What did he want, James?"

"It's about the lawsuit . . . hey."

Sarah, sitting on the bed, wore a very flimsy piece of lingerie. The lamp behind her made it see-through.

What was happening? She looked great. But the timing . . . "You don't like?" she said, a little distressed when I looked away.

"Oh, no, I . . . " Now, when I couldn't see straight? After all these weeks? I motioned toward Keri's Sleeping Area, a first down away. Interposing was a wall two-thirds up the ceiling. Sound traveled. "What about . . ."

"We'll be quiet."

"She might walk in."

"She's sleeping. She fell asleep hitting the bed. James," Sarah said with a frown, "she completely runs my life. God forgive me if, just once, I'm not Supermom. Come to bed." Coyly she added, "I've got lots of surprises."

Once again that rock and a hard place. "Sarah, I've . . . got a headache."

"Oh, come on."

I did. Bluto headache.

"James, are you all right?"

I watched the room sway, then stop. "It's just one of those days," I said with a sigh.

"I'll rub your forehead."

I walked toward her. She grabbed my hand and pulled me onto the bed. I nearly fell on her.

"I don't know what it is, James," she whispered. "You're so much . . . sexier. Like you've got a secret, a dark intrigue. Like you're involved with some life-and-death dilemma . . . like a private eye."

Talk about woman's intuition. "I thought you hated that," I said.

"It's the fantasy. Like you risked your life but survived. Then got your lady. Took your lady."

"Took her?"

"She's yours to take. Take me, James."

That sounded film noir.

In the dimness I looked down. My recuperative powers were having a party. What do you know?

"Take me," Sarah moaned.

I'd always wondered exactly why I wanted to be a private eye.

CHAPTER
12

The next day was chilly and wet. To be expected. New York City's spring is a surprise a minute.

I noticed the chill when I opened my eyes and stared at the open window letting it in. Considerate Sarah knows I love morning air.

Sarah was gone. Her digital clock said 9:00 A.M., an hour after she and daughter usually washed, breakfasted, and left. So much for life in the fast lane. This king of beasts rose at a tempo and hour befitting his masterly station, that of the successfully self-employed.

I felt great. But enough of last night. Risk assessing sex will be left for a later date.

My concussion, as concussions go, had been mild. I got dressed, chopped up an apple, a pear, a banana, dropped them into the blender, added a cup of water, noisily puréed, and drank. Sufficiently sugar-fueled, I slipped into one of Sarah's oversized sweatshirts and walked out into the morning chill.

At my office I updated my fault tree.

Above MINDY KILLED BY CAB I wrote, ANDY PICARD RESPONSIBLE. Above that I wrote WHY?

If Mindy were a mule for Andy Picard, who augmented his income by selling cocaine, she might have been killed for several reasons. I wrote, KNOWING TOO MUCH. INHALING THE GOODS.

Mindy seemed anxious during our meeting at the Apollo, but certainly not drugged. We'd been there forty minutes. She hadn't escaped to the bathroom.

I drew a question mark above INHALING THE GOODS.

WHAT ABOUT KNOWING TOO MUCH? Her telling me about her paranoia concerning the police seemed to negate that. If she was carrying drugs, why even mention the police?

Had Mindy been set up? Given a briefcase to deliver by dear Andy without knowing what was in it? I circled that as the most probable route.

And then had she discovered the setup? Or had Andy imagined she did? On my probability scale of ten, I gave that second choice an eight.

Do drug dealers off their ladies in borrowed taxicabs? That possibility got a three.

I had a Monte Carlo program on Mad Max that

could crunch probabilities if I fed it sufficient numbers (a Monte Carlo program figures the odds for every probability by sheer force). I didn't have sufficient numbers.

At least I had numbers above the three level. I also had more information about Brickman, specifically the hot new product and a public offering for the company producing it. AIDS self-test. To the side of THOMAS BRICKMAN RESPONSIBLE, I wrote PUBLIC OFFERING INVOLVING BIG BUCKS.

People do kill for money.

To get more information about that, and also about Andy Picard, a man in the business of promoting stocks as well as controlled substances, I went to visit a blood brother in risk.

My stockbroker.

Stockbrokers are risk assessors, pure and simple. They use one of the oldest forms of risk assessing around, the five-thousand-year-old technique of plus and minus, developed in Babylon, circa 3200 B.C., by a group of priests called the Asipu. Instead of studying the steaming entrails of goats, the usual means of coming to conclusions at the time, these earliest risk assessors, for a fee, helped clients tally up the pluses or minuses of a choice.

Stockbrokers do the same, predicting how far your stocks will soar or plummet.

Of course, those intent on making Salesmen of the Month don't tell you about the plummet part.

"Dr. Risk! It's Dr. Risk!" a broker shouted as I

got off the elevator high above Wall Street at the offices of Harrigan, Harrigan and Limm. This small but reputable firm employs my broker, Chuck Houlihan. I keep reminding Chuck he learned risk theory at my knee, but actually, like most stockbrokers, he got his face shoved in it by that perennially mean-spirited bully known as the Market.

The walls at Harrigan are burnished wood, the paintings hanging on them Elysian landscapes of the English countryside and fox hunts. That's what the client sees.

The risk assessor? He slips into the trading room, where the money to pay for these paintings is clawed out of human hides.

The trading room at Harrigan resembles a prison commissary. Long benches serve as communal desks. Retail and institutional brokers, crammed together, virtually sitting on one another's laps, shout, moan, laugh, cry, eat, and, most of all, phone.

"Hey, what the fuck's happening to Philip Morris?" someone screamed. You don't need drumbeats to know you're in a jungle. "Piece of shit, it should die of cancer and suck my dick!"

"There are ladies present," I whispered . . . to Judy Ann, the lady broker shouting this.

"How's it hanging, Doc?" Judy said with a smile.

"Well," I cried, amazed. "Yours?"

"The doctor is in, the doctor is in!" someone

hollered, and several brokers applauded. I was recently here to explain portfolio risk theory, invented by economist Harry Markowitz, Nobel Prize–winner.

But more important to this troop, I occasionally explain the nuances on the football and basketball spreads. These guys and gals bet on anything that writhes.

I made my way into Chuck's glass-enclosed office, payoff to him for top dog in commissions. Chuck, as usual, was hard at work, scribbling on the *Post* crossword puzzle. "Related to an orangutan," he said. "Related to an orangutan. Six letters."

"Chuck, can't you say hello?"

"Starts with an S."

"Simian?"

He printed the letters in ballpoint, then looked up and smiled. "How are you doing?"

Entering Harrigan's is always unsettling.

"Hey, did you hear the one about the two gay guys in a bar?" Chuck asked. Though he swears he's unprejudiced—in his eyes all colors and creeds get equal desecration—Chuck's bad joke repertoire is nearly as large as Beelzebub's. "Two gay guys at a bar. What does one say to the other?"

"Chuck, I don't want to hear."

Chuck shrugged. "You sure?" The phone rang. Chuck ignored it. "Okay. Want some chili?" I noticed a styrofoam container of chili on his desk. It was ten in the morning. "Spicy spicy. You'll like it."

"No, thanks."

So," he said, "forgive me for living. I can't interest you in my politically incorrect jokes or my chili. What brings you here?"

"Can I find out if Andy Picard, a stockbroker, had any work-related problems?"

Chuck took a bite of his chili. "Sure. Call the SEC's eight hundred number. They'll say if he has complaints on his U-five."

"U-five?"

"Some form."

"He works for Pesky and Rashowitz," I said.

"He's got complaints," Chuck said. "They're whoredom's biggest whore."

"Do they bring out new issues?"

"They bring out penny stocks. They bring out fairy tales and optical illusions."

"They're not the brokers for Healers?"

Chuck thought a moment. "Healers? You're interested in Healers?"

"Yes," I said.

"Pesky and Rashowitz couldn't get two shares of Healers. Forget Healers. I've got a lot better. Hillary Chicken."

"Hillary Chicken?"

"You get two huge thighs, two tiny breasts, and seven left wings. Okay, Healers," he said, smirking at my lack of response. "Hey, Tony!" he shouted out his open door, nearly popping my eardrums. "You got a prospectus on Healers?"

The hue and cry was taken up by several other brokers. Someone threw a forty-page prospectus halfway across the room. I ducked as it got tossed into the office. "Good thing your clients don't see this," I said.

"This is nothing. At Argyle one guy walks across the trading floor in his boxer shorts. Here." And Chuck started to read the pertinent information of the prospectus of Healers Inc., stock symbol HEEL.

"New issues" like Healers Inc., in case you're unaware, are private companies that "go public"—in short, they allow the public, including you and me, to own them. Apple Computer was once privately owned, as was IBM, and they too, in "going public," had "offerings," "underwritten" by brokerage firms to help sell their shares, which the public learned about through a "prospectus," a booklet full of information scrutinized by the Securities and Exchange Commission to make sure the companies told the truth and nothing but.

Why do private companies "go public"? A public offering can raise lots of cash.

"It's coming in two weeks, probably at six," Chuck said. "Five million shares. Hope you don't want some."

"Why?"

"It's hot as a firecracker."

"Who's the boss?" I asked, looking over Chuck's shoulder.

Chuck turned a page. "Thomas Brickman. Friend of yours?"

"How many shares does he own?"

Chuck turned another page and pointed. "One million, eight hundred thousand, and seventy three."

At six dollars per that would yield north of ten million dollars. Not bad for a day's work. "When can he sell them?"

"Two years after the offering."

Two years and a ten-million-dollar windfall. Oh, doctor.

"How can I stop the deal?" I asked.

Chuck read the prospectus some more, then put it down. He stared at me. He picked up his styrofoam container of chili and thoughtfully chewed a plastic spoonful. "This is good."

"I'm serious. How can it get stopped?"

"Are you aware of something I'm not?"

I told him I was involved in a detective case.

Now Chuck is a veteran of several world wars, all occurring during the average day at the stock market. He's seen too much money lost too quickly with too much bleeding. If I told him I'd just shot the pope, he'd react, as he did now, with that cautious, hooded stare that said, "I'll believe anything for ten minutes."

"You're a detective?"

"Right."

More stare. "Sam Spade or Lew Archer?"

"Plain Dr. Risk."

Chuck nodded. I spotted a tiny, approving grin. "Well, good for you. And you want to know how a public offering gets stopped in its tracks?"

I nodded.

He dipped the spoon into the cup of chili, came up with an acidic clump, and chewed. "Fraud. Fraud can stop it."

"What kind?"

"Lying on the prospectus. For instance, like they made so much profit, only it's fudged."

"Involving Brickman?"

Chuck spent twenty more seconds skimming. "Especially that. He's a major part of the deal, with all these titles. Here it talks about loss of services." Chuck pointed to a page under a section entitled "Risks." "The company's based on goodwill. His good name."

I took a look. "So if Brickman's lying or doing something underhanded, that would stop it?"

"Something major. Very major."

Max, the sales manager, walked in. "Chuckie, that the chili? Give me a bite."

Chuck handed over the container. Max shoved in a mouthful.

"What about murder?" I said.

Max stared. "Yeah, that's what this is, murder." He left the office with the chili.

"Am I speaking English, Chuck? Would murder stop the offering?" I said.

Chuck stared at me. He stared some more. "What you're asking is, Would murder murder the issue?"

"I'm serious about this."

"That's what worries me."

"Chuck, I think Brickman murdered a woman. I'm gathering proof. Find out what you can about Andy Picard and call me, okay? I need to know."

I walked out. I noticed Chuck staring oddly after me.

"Adios, el doctor!" someone shouted in the trading room. A paper airplane floated by my head. I folded the prospectus and hurried out to enter the quiet of varnished walls and aristocratic paintings. A blue-veined dowager sat with her prep school grandson, waiting for her broker to come out and smile. You could hear a clock tick. Or the coupons being clipped from her bonds.

I preferred the illusion too.

CHAPTER
13

I spent the next couple of hours in my office, staring at the prospectus.

A ten-million-dollar stock deal. There was motive galore. Ten million reasons to take a risk.

Risk assessors measure risks to human life in dollars and cents. Since the dawn of time a pound of flesh has been valued in pennyweights, shekels, or pairs of goats.

It still is.

Federal law mandates you and I get a dollar value, to see how much money the government should spend to protect us. The EPA says we're each worth one and a half million dollars; OSHA, between two and five million (after adjustments for inflation).

Divide the ten-million-dollar stock deal by Mindy and Dave Washburn, and you got five million per person, the upper end of that OSHA estimate. This kind of division makes eminent sense to risk assessors as well as the criminal mind.

After reading the prospectus, I also realized something was wrong with this AIDS self-test.

Let me go on record. I'm all for self-tests, especially in the privacy of your home. With no one around you can find out what you want and take responsibility for your own health.

That wasn't the problem. The problem was, nothing is perfect.

I know that's perfectly obvious. It's perfectly obvious with medical tests too. No medical test is perfect, and the medical profession calls their screwups false positives or false negatives. Risk theorists call them deviations.

Whatever you call them, they exist.

Here's an example. The late, great writer Anthony Burgess got diagnosed with terminal brain cancer. In response he typed out his first novel, hoping to achieve immortality before the grim reaper knocked on his door.

The grim reaper never knocked. Burgess was misdiagnosed. (We've got all his books as a thank-you for that false positive.)

Medical tests fail. In fact, a requirement of

each medical test is a predicted rate at which it will fail. If a test fails 3 percent of the time, we say it has a 3 percent false positive rate.

That 3 percent is pretty good. Mammograms fail 10 to 20 percent of the time.

Brickman's AIDS self-test had a 97.8 percent accuracy, or a 2.2 percent false positive rate. Pretty good, you'd think.

Except for a fly in the ointment.

I'm going to approach this round about. Hang on.

Do you know what happens if you test positive for HIV? Your blood is tested again. Another positive, and there's a third test, the Western blot test or an immunofluorescent assay, to confirm the original results. With each test the false positive rate shrinks toward statistical insignificance.

Usually those taking this test are of the high-risk group. Why test if you're not?

But suppose you're not. Suppose you're in a low-risk group, very low. Can that affect the accuracy of the test?

We're going to talk Bayes Theorem. Don't hold your nose. It won't be like castor oil.

The Bayes Theorem deals with relational risks. *Relational* means "first risk first, second risk second."

Example: I buy a pregnancy test that's 99% accurate at the drugstore and go to the bathroom and pee on the little device, and, lo and behold, one of the pink dots, an indication of conception, disappears. Am I pregnant?

I don't think so.

If my stomach swells up and I start vomiting, I still won't think so. I'm a man. Only in the *National Enquirer* do men get pregnant.

But the test says I'm pregnant. And the test's accurate ninety-nine of one hundred times.

Obviously this kit is the faulty 1 percent. Obviously. I'm not going to get pregnant, no matter what.

But what if a woman, taking oral contraceptives, tests? The odds of her getting pregnant can be as small as 0.1 percent per year (though not as small as mine). If she tests positive, is it ninety-nine to one she's pregnant?

No.

Risks are relational. And separate. The risk of pregnancy and the risk of a bogus test are two different things.

Let's go back to those oral contraceptive–swallowing women. An 0.1 percent risk means that on average, one of one thousand will get pregnant each year.

But a thousand pregnancy tests will produce ten false positives (one of one hundred tests will give the wrong result). So, of a thousand of these women taking that pregnancy test, only one will be pregnant. But ten will test positive. That's a whopping 90 percent false positive! In short, take the pill, test positive, and it's nine to one you're not.

With AIDS the numbers get even crazier. If you're an American Caucasian adult with, over the years, only a few heterosexual lovers and no record of drug use, only one of fifty thousand of you will be HIV positive.

But one of ninety-eight AIDS self-tests will be wrong.

Meaning there will be 1,100 false positives in this group with only 1 true positive. Meaning the real chance of anyone in this group who tests HIV positive being positive is 1 in 1,100. That's a 99.9 percent false positive rate! That's 1,099 to 1 you don't have AIDS!

With that kind of accuracy, why take the test at all?

Good question.

Still, a 1,099 to 1 chance of a slow, painful death is not entirely insignificant. As a risk theorist, aware of the numbers, I might mention this at my annual checkup, if I remember.

What would you do?

You'd probably start sweating profusely, wildly grab the directions, read the false positive number, and think, *My God, it's ninety-seven out of a hundred I'm dying of AIDS!* And spend the next several days, weeks, or months fighting depression.

Or maybe you'd kill yourself.

And all for a diagnosis that's almost positively wrong.

I read in the prospectus that FDA approval was

"imminent." Enough bad publicity, and denial would be imminent.

Brickman had to know about the Bayes Theorem. He had to know about the nightmares that might accompany his self-test.

That brought me back to Mindy Sayles. What did this have to do with her? Or Andy Picard? Or Dave Washburn?

I hadn't a clue.

An hour later, after a grand repast of Chinese from my favorite takeout, I called Grimes. He picked up after the first ring.

"Lieutenant," I said, "it's James Denny. Dr. Risk."

"Oh."

That didn't sound wildly enthusiastic. "My head's much better," I said. A pause. No congratulations?

"I'm busy, James," he finally said.

Busy when I was cracking the case? "But, Lieutenant, I've got something hot."

"Hot as that clipping?"

The clipping! The newspaper clipping Mindy mentioned before she was killed, *Boston Herald*, thirty years old, April! "Did you find it?"

"Find it? You're asking if I found it?"

Talking to Grimes was kind of like trick or treat. "Well, yes, I did ask . . ."

"I had a researcher go to the Public Library, at great expense," Grimes said, "look through all those long-ago *Boston Herald*s."

"And?"

"Found nothing."

"What do you mean?"

"You don't know what *nothing* means, James? *Nada*? Zip?"

"Oh, that nothing," I said.

"Nothing about Brickman"—Grimes continued glumly—"Mindy Sayles, Dave Washburn, Andy Picard. Nothing about doctors. Sculptures. The guy filed six hours. Thirty days of *Herald*s with a fine-tooth comb."

"Nothing," I repeated dully.

"I'm still getting crap," Grimes said.

Well, this was a setback. I had expected . . . I didn't know what I'd expected, but it wasn't nothing. "I've got information," I offered.

"Don't want it."

"Lieutenant"—I continued, determined—"Brickman owns major shares—"

"Still don't want it."

"—in a stock deal. It's happening next week."

"Stock deal? Stock deal?" Grimes repeated.

"Yes," I said, perplexed.

"Well, James, there's a connection. Remember Washburn? That guy we found in Mindy Sayles's loft? He was involved with stock deals."

"What do you mean?"

"He was hired by someone affiliated with Securities and Exchange."

I stared at the phone in my hand. "Stock fraud!" I cried. "Stock fraud with Brickman!"

"Brickman?" Tony Grimes said. "This has nothing to do with Brickman. This has to do with Andy Picard."

"Thomas Brickman!" I repeated.

There was silence on the line. "James," Grimes said slowly, "Andy Picard is a stockbroker, remember? The SEC has jurisdiction—."

"The SEC's not interested in a drug deal. What else did they tell you?" I asked.

"James . . ."

"Lieutenant, I have to know."

"They told me nothing."

"Nothing?"

"The information's restricted," Grimes answered.

"Their guy got killed!"

"James," Grimes said.

"Lieutenant, listen. Mindy found something. Washburn too. Implicating Brickman."

But whatever they found wasn't in that clipping. There was no clipping. Or maybe I'd gotten it wrong. Maybe it was thirty-one years ago. Maybe it was March. Maybe Mindy had spoken in tongues.

"James," Grimes said wearily, "I've got to go."

"Lieutenant, there are too many coincidences. Too many knots in the loose ends, don't you see? Look, I'll call back when I'm clear on this, okay?"

"Don't call back, James," Grimes said softly. "We're the police. We'll do this all by ourselves."

"I'll call back," I said, and hung up.

CHAPTER
14

Of course it was the stock deal! It had to be.

Why would the SEC be interested in Picard? It didn't need a private eye to investigate a drug deal. Drug dealing was for a different kind of police.

On my blackboard I wrote, above THOMAS BRICKMAN RESPONSIBLE, DAVE WASHBURN INVESTIGATING AIDS SELF-TEST STOCK DEAL.

Investigating what?

I skimmed the prospectus for Healers Inc. It had the usual warnings about future profits, potential problems, the speculative nature of the beast. I probably wasn't going to find any obvious scandal here.

I did find another Brickman.

On page three of the prospectus was a listing

127

of the board of directors for Healers Inc. Up there under Brickman's name was Julie Brickman, the good doctor's wife.

I phoned Chuck. "Hello, Chuck?"

"Hello, Chuck?"

"Chuck, I . . ."

"Chuck, I . . ."

I forgive Chuck his alleged sense of humor. It's an antidote for crack-up when stock market risk assessment runs amok. "I need your help," I said.

"Okay, but I heard nothing on Picard."

I told Chuck I was interested in Julie Brickman.

"Her being on the board is no big deal," he explained. "In closely held companies, you do what you want. Brickman could make her Exchequer of the Ladies' Room, just to pay her a salary."

"Would she know anything about Healers?"

"She might show for board meetings, things like that. She'd vote the way he tells her. Sorry I can't help more. Hey, hear the one about the Irishman in the London bar with a talking parrot?"

"Chuck, I got to run."

"Bartender says, 'Where'd you get that?' Parrot says, 'Dublin.' "

I hung up.

Above BRICKMAN on my blackboard I wrote, HITS WOMEN. He had hit Mindy. Abusing women isn't a one-time thing.

The odds of a woman beater being a wife beater were pretty good. So I decided to get in contact with Julie Brickman. If her husband was abu-

sive, I might find an ally on the board of directors
of Healers Inc.

"Julie Brickman, I presume?" I rehearsed this
approach in my mind the next morning as I sat in a
park opposite the doctor's Upper East Side apartment near Gracie Mansion. I was hiding behind a
New York Times, fueling my nerves with a container of coffee and a buttered bagel from a nearby
deli, and waiting to match a photograph of Julie
Brickman I'd downloaded from a graphics bulletin
board with any woman walking past the doorman.

Searching state records on the Internet, I'd discovered that Julie Brickman née Darrow hailed
from Dallas. Mid-thirties now, she'd married Brickman a decade ago at the height of a print modeling
and occasional acting career. I had gotten her former big-deal agency to fax me a copy of old head
and body shots. The faxes stressed the all-Ameri-
can girl next door, apple pie, pigtails, freckles, L'il
Abner's Daisy. Homespun innocence hiding lots of
sex appeal.

But by ten o'clock nobody like that had appeared. I'd read everything in the *Times* and even
prepared myself to do battle with the crossword
puzzle when a woman in a jogging suit and dark
glasses and carrying a book bag walked past her
doorman.

Even without the identifying photo, you could

tell by the walk. It had a natural elegance we normal clumsy folks lack. This might have had something to do with Julie Brickman's legs; they were longer than a small giraffe's.

After casually dropping my paper container and brown bagel bag containing half a bagel in a wire wastebasket, and folding my paper like any other purposeful New Yorker, I followed right behind.

My training in the fine art of tailing the suspect was grainy black-and-white movies. Humphrey Bogart and James Cagney emitting lots of dirty looks. Flicking their cigarette butts over their shoulders.

Those were the movies. This was real life.

But in New York City nobody looks at anybody for more than a second anyway. So I was as safe as a Hollywood shamus.

She walked; I followed.

At the corner I stopped a yard or two behind as she waited for the light. Five feet ten and gazing down large dark glasses, she seemed haughty, aristocratic, with no affection for the hoi polloi.

The light changed. She walked; I followed.

My plan? To wait for the right moment to approach. Okay, the "ideal moment." The "right moment" had passed half a dozen times during the previous five minutes. Well, I kind of felt like I was picking her up, which made me shy.

Picking her up?

I wasn't used to this.

I courageously approached at a semi-ideal moment in front of a cheese store. "Julie Brickman?" I said, omitting the "presume."

She turned, startled, and peeked above those dark glasses.

"Mrs. Brickman, I'm James Denny," I continued, extending my hand. "Can we talk?"

She continued staring. She hadn't a clue.

"Mrs. Brickman, I'm investigating your husband in connection with a lawsuit brought by my client."

That got a response. The wrong one. She froze up, then looked around wildly.

And started to run.

I stood, flat-footed. Of all the possible scenarios I'd come up with, this was completely unexpected. I'd asked an innocuous question, in my opinion, and she'd taken off like a deer. In fact I felt I'd done something wrong, that I should run, in an opposite direction.

When she jogged toward Ninety-first Street, my brain revived. "Wait!" I cried, and raced after her.

Luckily the spontaneous, graceful walk of a model didn't translate into an efficient sprint. I easily caught her beside parked cars and piled-up garbage bags. An elderly couple, clinging to each other, had inadvertently blocked her way.

I grabbed the sleeve of her jogging suit. The elderly couple nervously brushed past. "Mrs. Brickman, please," I said, panting. The sun was in my eyes. "I just want to talk."

"Who are you?"

"You don't know me. I want to talk about Healers Inc. Is there anything shady about that? Do you know anything about a clipping from the *Boston Herald*?"

"Who are you?" she repeated, shaking her head nervously. Her dark glasses slipped down her nose.

And there, revealed behind the glasses, was a purple eye puffed to the size of a walnut.

Apparently she had forgotten what she looked like, for she continued to stare, uncomprehending. Then her hand came up, felt the glasses, and pushed them back.

"Did he do that?" I cried.

"I don't know you," she whispered.

"Did he hit you?"

"Are you the police?"

"I represent Mindy Sayles. Did he?"

The name Mindy Sayles stopped her. She spit out angrily, "A woman!," then pulled her arm away.

"A woman he murdered," I said.

Julie Brickman stared some more, then turned and started running down the street again.

"Mrs. Brickman!" I cried. I took a step. Should I chase and harass her more?

The hell with it. I walked to the corner. When I turned, she was gone.

On York Avenue the usual suspects were out, enjoying this lovely spring morning. I scuffled slowly toward Brickman's building. At the entrance I stared at the doorman, who glared back. Perhaps, running into the lobby, Julie had described me.

The doorman stopped scowling for a moment to look at my card. "For Mrs. Brickman," I said with a shrug. He snatched it.

I walked back to the park to gather my thoughts.

Brickman had probably given his wife that eye. But why hit her? To keep her mouth shut about Healers? The clipping? Because he had a bad-hair day?

I sat down on the concrete bench. Too much information bubbled in my head.

I got up and walked to the wastebasket and searched inside for my half bagel. What do you know? It was still there. With New York's hungry homeless population, what were the odds of that?

I walked over to a phone booth and dialed my answering machine. What do you know? Nothing there.

I hung up, then just listened to the dial tone for a moment. It brought back a memory.

I remembered speaking to Mindy by phone and hearing something unusual on the line. A static clicking. Mindy said she was being followed, and there was a private investigator at her loft. Private investigators and phone surveillance go hand in glove.

I put a quarter in the phone again. I waited. "Richie?" I said. "It's Dr. Risk."

Richie Teller is the owner of the Spying Store, that ingenious shop down on West Street that sells electronic bugging and debugging devices. My incessant browsing has made us friends. "Yo, bro?" I heard.

"Richie, what's the sound of a phone being tapped?"

"You mean, what's the sound of one phone tapping?"

"I'm serious."

"What kind of phone?"

What kind of phone did Mindy have? I closed my eyes and pictured her loft. "Cordless!" I cried.

"Okay," Richie said. "Two sounds. One is an intermittent tap. That's why it's called tapping. If there's a physical bug on the premises—"

"Physical?"

"Something you click on the line or the terminal box, then attach to headsets, tape recorder—"

"What's the other sound?"

"For cordless? A rhythmic clicking. Like a static machine."

That was what I'd heard in my office on the phone!

"A cordless works on radio waves," Richie continued. "To tap that, you need a scanning receiver and a kind of computer to search through the different bands."

"You need a lot of hardware?"

"Maybe a CB receiver, an antenna, a Mac. Oh, yeah, a place to store and move it. In this city, more than a thousand feet and all you hear is noise."

A place to store and move it. I closed my eyes and pictured something outside Mindy's loft. "How about a van?" I cried. "Could you store it in a van?"

"Perfect," Richie said.

A van with funny plates! Delaware plates, I'd put odds on, the state of residence of Dave Washburn. A van parked on the street near Mindy's loft (the parking rules in TriBeCa are fairly lax) that Dave Washburn couldn't drive off after inhaling the stench of a thousand rotten eggs.

I hailed a cab. I would have asked the doorman, but doubted the scope of his sense of humor. In the backseat I tried to explain to a newly transplanted Siberian cabbie named Ilyivich how to get to TriBeCa, pronto.

CHAPTER
15

This was the piece of the puzzle that never fit.

Obviously Dave Washburn was in the Apollo coffee shop with Mindy and me. Obviously he'd given me the note to give to Mindy, then stood and watched as she was hit by the cab. Obviously he'd raced back downtown to her loft, had got himself inside, and got himself dead.

But how had he gotten to the Apollo before Mindy and I did? Was it a lucky accident? Random chance?

Of course he had to know we were going there. And the only ways to know would be (1) to have telepathic powers or (2) the ability to overhear our plans made on the phone fifteen minutes prior to our meeting.

Phone surveillance.

It was about noon when Ilyivich finally got past midtown traffic, several inexplicable detours, and a shouting match with a bicyclist—I'm telling you, it's in the genes—to let me out beside the building that housed Mindy's loft. He offered no thanks for my generous tip except a Slavic curse, then drove into the perpetual winter of his Russian soul.

I turned to the business at hand.

As I said, parking rules are lax here. Some of the signs are blacked out, so folks can sometimes park where and when they wish.

I turned a corner. We were a block away from Mindy's loft, less than a thousand feet. There were four cars and a motorcycle parked along the curb.

And a van with the funny license plates.

Delaware plates!

I walked around it. Nothing unusual. The antenna was removed, a common precaution on these mean city streets. A sign on the van warned of a high-class security system, lest you foolishly jimmy the door.

I foolishly jimmied. No siren. I went around to the back and gave the handle a tug.

The door opened.

And there, revealed inside, was a virtual surveillance studio, with tape decks, oscillators, transmitters, two Macintosh computers, a small sound mixer, headsets, in short, all the fixings needed to bug the former Kremlin and the current Pentagon combined.

For Mindy's cordless this was overkill.

I cautiously climbed inside. Cautiously, for this risk assessor was cautious by occupation and nature. But also, why was the door open and the alarm system shut? Was someone about to return to find a bear sleeping in his bed?

I turned on an overhead light with a handkerchief. All this shiny plastic might be covered with prints. With my hankie I very carefully searched for tapes, disks, and so forth, but a disturbing conclusion occurred. There weren't any. The disk drives were empty, the cassette decks ejected.

Plus there were no signs of tampering. Either an extraordinary locksmith with a degree in electronics hot-wired the alarm, or the person who took the tapes and, oddly, left the door open, had Washburn's keys.

The man who had killed Washburn. Yes!

Nothing had been found on the poisoned Washburn except some credit cards. No receipts for meals or bus tickets or parking lots. No keys, not even house keys.

Where were all these things? Obviously someone had gone through Washburn's pockets in Mindy's loft, then come here, disarmed the alarm, opened the door, and took taped evidence of phone conversations of Mindy Sayles.

Who?

Thomas Brickman? Someone he'd hired? Charley's Aunt?

The probabilities were small on Charley's Aunt.

I climbed out of the van and started to cross the street. I stopped. My shoes got stuck on some kind of gunk, some oil-based residue. You've got to watch your step in this dog pound of a city. Too many people and pets and crap jammed into the size of a toilet stall . . .

Was this King Kong's bubble gum? I raised the sole of my shoe. A brownish puddle surrounded me. Where'd that come from? The stuff oozed like an oil leak.

This wasn't oil.

I stooped, pressed my hands on the asphalt, and peered under the chassis. My hair stood on end. That's not entirely accurate. The hair on my head sat where I'd combed it this morning. The hair on my arms, my neck, the fine hairs that cover the human body, that lovely mammalian down that reminds us of our connection to hirsute forebears, that hair stood at attention, as if some never-dead swamp thing had brushed up against me.

Under the van near the driveshaft were three eyes, wide open. Two were white, and the third, the mythical third, from which all universal knowledge derives, was brown. It took me a while to realize that rather than the source of eternal wisdom, this third eye was a hole where a bullet had entered Andy Picard's brain.

CHAPTER
16

I phoned in this murder from the same phone booth. Déjà vu. Somebody other than Lieutenant Grimes picked up.

"He isn't in?" I cried. "But I found a dead body!"

"Call 9-1-1."

Great advice.

I did. No one arrived for twenty minutes. Well, Andy wasn't going anywhere.

Twenty minutes after that Grimes roared by in his unmarked car.

"Lieutenant Grimes!" I shouted. Two squad cars had preceded him, their red lights flashing. An EMS van whined in the distance, on its way.

"What are you doing here, James?" Grimes

said, walking up to the back of the van and sighing mightily. He stuck his head in.

I peered over his shoulder. The other cops were snapping photos, setting up that yellow crime tape, dusting for prints. "What am I doing?" I repeated. An odd question. "Lieutenant, I found—"

Grimes turned. "Don't tell me what you found. What are you doing here? I told you to leave the physical shit!"

"Physical—"

"All of it!"

Why was Grimes so mad? Here I was, helping him crack the case.

"I just got off the phone getting screamed at. Screamed at!" Grimes shouted, breathing fire.

"What do you mean?"

"About Brickman. Him, him!"

Brickman, it seemed, had just called Lieutenant Grimes's captain to report a wife recently harassed. The captain called Grimes.

I looked at my feet.

"He's getting a court order: we come near her, our butts get sued."

My shoes were scuffed. They could use a shine. "Brickman called your captain?" I asked.

"Somebody else. It doesn't matter."

"How can he call a captain? Does he have so much clout?"

"Doesn't matter!" he cried. "It came back to me."

"Well, it seems unusual." I had this feeling I'd

better change the subject. "Brickman beat her up," I offered. "His wife."

"I don't care if he gang-banged her and the ladies' auxiliary! What kind of shit are you pulling? You're fucking up my case."

They were driving a tow truck to lift the van over dead Andy. They had now hooked the tow bar onto the front end. "Well," I said, taking a breath to recover, "I don't see how I'm doing that."

"Oh, you don't, do you? Well, maybe you're not. Maybe it's me."

I said nothing. I had no idea what problems he was having with his higher ups.

"Anyway, it's a drug deal," Grimes said. "Nothing more."

"Why?"

"Why? What do you mean, why? Picard was dirty."

"Picard?"

"The guy who's dead. The stiff."

"I know who he is."

"Well, what you don't know is he sells to everyone at his office. His clients, his bosses. The SEC's interested in drugs in the industry, so they send Washburn to look. He follows Mindy Sayles, one of Andy's mules—"

"He tapped her phone?"

"Who?"

"Dave Washburn."

"Why not?"

"There were no tapes."

"Hey, someone took them. But he's got the equipment to."

"Why was Picard killed?"

"Drug-related."

"Why was he killed here?"

"It's drugs, okay?" Grimes said with a groan, as if this should explain everything. "Drugs. Half the murders in this city have to do with drugs."

Actually the number was higher, but I didn't feel a factoid was appropriate now. "Lieutenant," I said, "there are too many loose ends. Too many fluctuations."

"Fluctuations?"

"The note? You know, 'We're Watching!'?"

Grimes gnawed on his lower lip.

"They weren't watching Picard. It was Brickman they were watching," I said. "Brickman's stock deal is going down."

The tow truck had now raised the van and was slowly dragging it away from the body. Andy and his third eye glared up at the sky in accusation. Somebody tell the truth, he seemed to say.

"This doesn't connect to Brickman," Grimes muttered. "How many times do I have to say that?"

"Is Brickman putting pressure on the department?"

"You've got no evidence it connects to Brickman! Nothing. Do you have one piece of goddamn evidence?"

"Not exactly," I said.

A news crew had parked down the street, presenting the police with one more problem of murder in public places. A reporter with an accompanying cameraman walked toward the body. A detective hustled over to intercept.

"By the way," Grimes said, looking straight ahead, "say one word to those shitheads and I'm stuffing you in the bag with the stiff."

The detective pushed the media troop back.

"I'm not going to talk," I said. "Why would I talk?"

"Why do you do anything? *You* don't know."

The man was not getting with my program. "Lieutenant, Brickman has a ten-million-dollar stock deal. He stopped the people who could have stopped it—Mindy, Washburn, Picard."

"How could they stop it?"

"I don't know."

A small crowd had gathered, even in this forlorn part of Manhattan. Death attracts. "You don't know," Grimes said, shaking his head. "You don't know why Washburn went to Mindy's loft. Or why Andy's here. Or why or even if anyone killed anyone. You don't know because it's a drug deal. Plain and simple, a drug deal!"

"Except for the clipping."

A murderous gleam came into Grimes's eyes. He bit both lips alternately, possibly his way of counting to ten. He started walking to the van.

"I'm serious," I cried, following him.

"I'm not saying shit now," he muttered, not looking at me.

"Your researcher didn't know what to look for. I'll meet you tomorrow. At the Public Library. Can you make it?"

"What?" Grimes turned, bewildered. "You want me to what?"

"Tomorrow. At eleven. The Reading Room on the third floor. We'll search together."

"Nuts, the man is nuts," he cried, and started walking again.

"It's risk theory. Chance error," I said, following him. "Tests have a margin of error. To be certain, you rerun them." I was out on a wing and a prayer with Grimes on this one.

"Tests?"

"Your man at the library didn't know what to look for. The odds of his finding the clipping weren't a lock."

Grimes stopped. He looked at his feet, as if amazed they'd wouldn't maneuver him past this source of fantastic irritation. "The man's serious. You're serious."

"Mistakes happen. He didn't see what he should."

The news crew, with Andy as a distant backdrop, started shooting a report. A familiar-looking woman gestured and spoke into a mike.

"He missed it, that's what you're saying? The man missed the clipping?"

"He didn't have enough information to go on."

"He said no mention of Brickman. No mention of Sayles."

"Maybe they changed their names."

"Maybe they're pumpkins and little white mice. Maybe at midnight they get to be Cinderella!"

This discussion was going nowhere. I started to walk away.

"Why can't you look yourself?" he shouted.

I turned back. "Two heads are better than one."

"Tomorrow's my day off!"

My attention got caught by the remains of Andy Picard. The EMS troop stood like vultures as a medical examiner poked around the corpse while dictating into a tiny recording device.

"It won't take long," I said.

"I'm spending the day with my kid, you hear!"

But I'd lost interest in Grimes.

An EMS guy unzipped a big black body bag. The cameras kept shooting. I had an eerie thought, staring at this hasty interment, that if I'd made my serendipitous connection and got down here sooner, Andy Picard wouldn't be dead.

Everyone's entitled to a good deed now and then.

CHAPTER
17

Back at my office my answering machine blinked.
A message from Buzz. I dialed.

"Hello?"

"Dr. Risk. Time to visit."

"What happened?"

"We got Brickman's files."

I said nothing.

"Aren't you excited? It's only four days. I owe
those lawyers big time."

"I'll be there in a while," I said.

"You're the one in a hurry."

True. But I was exhausted. You see, finding yet
another dead body had knocked the wind out of
my sails.

Okay, it's true that risk theorists deal constantly with death. We're always calculating its chance of occurrence, to avoid its occurrence. But calculation rarely occurs with a corpse in your face.

This was too much, all at once. A week ago I was counting bees in a beehive. On E-mail.

Maybe I should reevaluate the occupation of private dick. Risk assessors do that, assess occupations by calculating and factoring in average wage, preferred location, and risk of on-the-job injury or death to come up with the perfect fit for a meaningful career.

My best guess on the rewards of private detecting? That Chinese curse: an interesting life.

And the risks? Fraying of nerves, overriding paranoia. Plus being flung into outer space by the centrifugal force of the merry-go-round I'd jumped on in my haste to leave my risk-free existence. There was a musical show entitled, *Stop the World —I Want to Get Off*. I felt like shouting, "Stop the risks, I want to get off!"

Instead I changed into a green golf shirt and an Oakland Athletics cap. I was about to change my socks and underwear too. Not that they were soiled. Just suffused with the weariness of real, in-your-face death.

Have an interesting life, motherfucker.

* * *

An hour later I entered Buzz's office. "Want a drink?" Buzz asked.

"Do I look like I need one? Sarah!"

Sarah sat sipping a beer. She wore a very sexy corduroy miniskirt with flats. Sarah's a tall girl, tall, lithe, lovely, and, to toss in a fourth alliterative, luscious, with a body that effectively turns me on. But what was this body doing here? "It's Friday," she said, getting up and giving me a kiss. She smelled of perfume and beer.

"You look stunning," I said, trying to grin.

"That's what I've been saying for the last fifteen minutes," Buzz said. "Stunning."

I looked at Buzz. He looked at me. "Stunning," we repeated.

"Is everything okay?" Sarah said.

I had mentioned to Buzz the need to keep Sarah uninformed of my project.

"Of course," Buzz said.

"Of course," I agreed.

"Well, I don't know . . . I just thought I'd come by," she said. "You know, say hello to Buzz, see how his ponytail's growing."

Buzz grinned effusively, grabbed the hair, and slung it around like a snake.

"I was in the neighborhood," she continued. "Got some sausage on Bleecker. A Zito's loaf."

I nodded.

"Did you forget tonight, James?"

Tonight? What was tonight? "Forget? Why would you think I'd forget?"

"He needs a drink," Buzz said. "Beer?"

I opted for a hairier dog, some of the Johnnie Walker Red that Buzz keeps under his desk for the sorts of emergencies that occur on Friday afternoons when sobriety after a frustrating week gets life-threatening. A real emergency was occurring now. Tonight? "Ice?" Buzz asked. Without getting up he whirled in his chair, opened the baby fridge behind him, and tore out a tray. He pressed the cubes from the plastic tray into my glass. I stirred with a finger and sipped. "You needed that," Buzz said.

"Yes," I said.

"Why?" Sarah asked.

We both sat dead still.

"Why do you need a drink?" she repeated.

"A drink? Who needs a drink?" I said, grinning and holding up the glass, which my "sip" had drained by half.

"It's just a joke," Buzz said.

"Right," I said.

"What happened today that you need a drink?" Sarah insisted.

Oh, Sarah, you risk-assessing bloodhound. You can sniff out danger a mile away. "Today?" I said. "Let me see. I made a couple of phone calls. Found a couple of factoids." Watched Andy Picard get scraped off the macadam.

"He's here for a lawsuit," Buzz said.

"Right," I said. "That's it. Mindy Sayles."

"We're suing a doctor," Buzz said.

"What doctor?"

I glared at Buzz. Sarah's former doctor, I didn't want to say. "Sarah, it's not important."

"It sounds dangerous, James."

"Dangerous? There's nothing dangerous. Why would you think this is dangerous?" Not only did my nose grow, but I got donkey ears. "What'd you do today that was dangerous?" I said to distract her. I pointed at the ancient Coca-Cola clock above Buzz's head that showed ten to five. "Where's Keri?"

Thunder. Explosions. "You forgot!" she cried.

"Forgot?"

"Tonight!"

"What do you mean?" I said, fighting for time. "Tonight?"

"The theater!" Buzz cried. Sarah and I both turned. Was he nuts? Like charades, Buzz raised his eyebrows and wiggled his ears, hoping for some tiny clue from me, a wink, a blink? "I thought he mentioned the theater," he continued maniacally.

"Buzz," Sarah said.

Then it rose in me, like a whale from cavernous depths. "Lincoln Center! We're going to Lincoln Center!"

This was out of the Marx Brothers.

"Why are we going?" Sarah said. "James, I asked you a question."

Why? "Well . . ."

"It's our anniversary. We met nine months ago."

Sarah and I met randomly, I like to say, at a bus stop on the East Side. We just started chatting. The odds of our getting this far at the time were several hundreds to one. The odds of our going any farther now seemed slimmer.

"Our anniversary. Of course. Happy anniversary," I said, standing. "Would you like this dance?"

Sarah turned away with a scowl. "Dance?"

"As it's our anniversary, would you like this anniversary dance."

"I knew you'd forget," she huffed as I helped her off the seat. "What do you mean, dance?"

"Buzz, 'The Anniversary Waltz,' please."

Buzz stared at me, then nodded and started humming. It was the "Tennessee Waltz." Who cared? Sarah grimaced, stiff as rubber sealant on a January morning. I clumsily waltzed her around. I had no clue if this was a waltz, as I'd never waltzed before. One, two, three, one, two, three, Buzz whacked on his desk, humming out of time, out of tune.

"All right, all right," Sarah said. There was a line of sweat over her upper lip.

"I'll bet I swept you off your feet, huh?" I said.

"Right," she said. As I grabbed my scotch and gulped it to oblivion, she looked deep into my lying eyes. "See you at seven," she said, grabbing her purse and the bagful of sausage. At the door she almost smiled at me but saved it for the azalea bushes.

I turned to Buzz when the door shut. "Buzz," I said. "More scotch."

More scotch to calm down. My new adventure didn't need Sarah viciously on my case.

"Tough lady," Buzz said, nodding.

I sighed. "Brickman was her doctor. That's one reason I don't want her to know."

"And the other reasons?"

"I don't want to talk about it."

I swirled the ice around, sniffed the bouquet, and got a satisfying bit of the poison between my lips. Naturally Sarah and I were on a collision course. Eventually she was going to find out, and eventually I was going to have to deal with that. Eventually. Now I just wanted to pay attention to how the room got brighter even with the sun declining. And how the traffic on Seventh Avenue, fifty yards away, sounded musical instead of just intense. Hordes of commuters, slamming on their brakes and pressing their horns, inched toward the tunnel, singing an erratic chorus of "Help!" I had this desire to sit in this twilight suffusing through Buzz's windows and, watching lights snap on like fireflies, get so righteously lit myself I couldn't walk. Drunk as a steamboat drifting toward China.

Instead I detailed to Buzz exactly how "interesting" things had become.

As I told about Julie Brickman and Andy

Picard, the man with three eyes, Buzz's smile got stuck. Though Buzz has heard many a wayward tale, this one was a doozy.

"You ought to go on a talk show," he said quietly when I'd finished. "Get a ghostwriter to write it."

"It's not a joke, Buzz. And, there are too many detours to believe this is simply a drug case. Mindy Sayles was scared of the cops. Someone into drugs doesn't tell you that. And why snoop in her loft?"

"Maybe Picard hired Washburn."

"Andy Picard had two huge zombies to do his dirty work. And why tap Mindy Sayles?"

"You said the SEC. Your Detective Grimes said they were following the stockbroker."

"Why snoop on Mindy? Why follow her? Why pass her a note to warn her?"

"You're the detective, not me," Buzz said. "Anyway, I don't see it with this Brickman guy. He's got no motive."

"Maybe these records," I said.

"You really think they'll show a motive to kill? A smart guy like him?"

"Then it's connected to the stock deal."

"That's a guess, James."

An educated guess, based on wayward probability. "He beat up his wife," I added. "The doctor who helps women beat up his wife."

"That doesn't make him a killer."

"More scotch?" I turned over my glass.

Buzz stared. "Look, it's just . . . why are you after this guy? What are you doing?"

"Getting shit-faced." I took the bottle and poured three fingers in, before the cubes.

"Sarah'll love that. Plus the fact you're leading a double life."

I sloshed the whiskey and ice around. "Well, she's not going to know unless you tell. Anyway, what should I do? Be risk-free? I was sick of that."

"Sounds like now you're risk-a-minute. Find a middle ground."

"In the long run I will. In the long run," I said with a sigh. In the long run risk theory seeks the middle ground. In the long run the roller coaster ride levels out.

In the short run it was the Mario Brothers and Mortal Combat combined.

Through the window across the way green ivy darkened. Gotham becoming Emerald City. Obviously you had to be there . . . drinking.

"So why are you really after this guy?" Buzz asked after a minute of silence.

"Because he's too perfect. Everything about him. His looks. His wife's looks. His career. Where does he come from? What made him this center-field monument? This imperious, impregnable big shot?"

"What is this, penis envy?"

"Utter amazement. He's perfect, and quite simply, perfection doesn't exist."

"It doesn't?"

"Not that I know of."

Buzz glared at me. "What about Ted Williams? Willie Mays?"

"That's your definition."

"Mine and civilization's."

"It's a definition. We're not talking definitions. Listen. Flip a coin ten times, perfect is five."

"What?"

Whiskey-sloshed as I was, I was determined to make a risk theory point. "Flip a coin ten times, what are the odds you get an equal amount?"

"You need more scotch." Buzz filled me up, then poured for himself.

I took a sip. "What are the odds of getting five heads?"

"Out of ten? Fifty-fifty?"

"One in three."

"Jesus Christ."

I thought he was exclaiming about this statistical revelation, but it was a water bug skittering across the floor. He grabbed a paperweight from his desk and, in a motion of pure, unimpeded violence, tossed it in that direction, where it banged on the floor, rolled over the bug with a splat, and smashed into the wall.

"Nice shot," I said.

"Thanks."

"Almost perfect." Nothing like scotch for helping you make a point. Also for tolerating a large water bug. "But for risk theorists, perfection isn't defined, it's measured. Like rolling a seven in craps ten times. Would you call that perfect?"

"If I were pressing fifty-dollar bets."

"What are the odds of rolling ten sevens?" Buzz moaned.

"Just listen. There are six combinations on two dice that equal seven. Six and one. Five and two. Four and three."

"I'm listening . . . that's three."

"Double them. Each die can have the opposite arrangement. Six ways to throw seven, and thirty not to—there are thirty-six ways two dice can fall —gives six out of thirty or one in five you're getting seven when you toss them bones."

"You're putting me to sleep."

"You'll get back at me later. Ten sevens in a row is one in five times itself ten times. One in five to the tenth power is . . . got a calculator?" Buzz groaned, reached down, and tossed one over. I punched in the numbers. "See, when I get drunk, I get sober enough to do this." More punching. I read the LCD answer. "Zero-point-zero-zero-zero-zero-zero-zero-one-zero-two-four. About one in ten million. Pretty slim, huh?"

"What the fuck are you talking about?" Buzz said.

"I'll tell you. Know what the casino'll do after you, the shooter, achieves such perfection?"

"Throw out the dice?"

"You bet. And not because they're sore losers. They know the improbability of perfection."

"So when something's so perfect . . ."

"Chances are real good it's a crock of shit."

Horns honked far away. Darkness wove a web on the ivy. Lights blinked in windows.

"He's a crock of shit?" Buzz asked.

"Absolutely."

Buzz nodded and ruminated on that. "So why are you really after this guy?" he finally said.

I sneered at Buzz.

But actually it was still a wonderful question. Why was I after Brickman? Because Mindy Sayles had extracted a pledge? Because my fear of a risk-free, adventure-free, excitement-free existence had made me desperate for a villain to pursue toward calamity?

Why was I after this guy?

"Let me look at his numbers," I said.

"Now?"

"Nah, I couldn't even see them. Where are they?"

He clumsily tossed me a folder full. Half the pages fell on the floor. I stooped, picked some up, and started scanning.

"Look, I got to go," Buzz said with a sigh. "Ellen's waiting." He looked over his head at the clock. "You've got an hour to sober up and get to Sarah's."

I groaned.

Outside, the cool air smelled full of promise. In the distance the outlines of cars got focused against a golden sky. Clouds mauve and pink, the buildings a rich rust color. The world seemed, for one second, perfect.

What the hell were the odds against that?

At Lincoln Center only occasionally did the balcony in Avery Fisher Hall feel like the bridge of a huge swaying ship.

Sarah didn't seem to notice. Apparently I'm good at hiding a total loss of control. She smiled a lot and looked around importantly, as if this momentous event were only admissible to blue-blooded relations of Miles Standish. Or Westchester folks with a cherished subscription.

Why do people go to these things? All this classical music has been done a billion times. Yes, occasionally they make a crescendo here instead of there. So what?

My grumpiness had to do with Brickman (plus a semihangover) and a gnawing sense of failure. If those records were kosher, as they very well might be, I'd be headfirst against a big-butt deadend.

But we had to hide all this—didn't we?—because this was Sarah's night. She'd done herself up for it exquisitely in a sparkling black mini, black mesh stockings, and step-on-me high heels. She looked as expectant and nervous as a warrior painted for battle. Against what was she battling? Some primitive anxiety created when Mom put on something similar. "Garter belt?" I'd asked earlier, and she'd winked, but I'd seen the toll taken, hours spent trying on things and shopping and parading before the mirror in what might seem to me a wonderful fashion show but to Sarah was a stroll through Hades, a jog through the netherworld, with this no good, that too short, that too fat.

Why do women dress up? For other women? Their fathers? Mythical Greek gods? Someone ought to do a risk assessment on a woman's loss of life expectancy caused by clothing anxiety.

"James, I'm talking to you."

"What?"

"Give me my ticket. I want to go to the ladies' room."

Amazingly I found the ticket in my pocket. I watched her squeeze past my knees and saunter up the aisle. What the hell. She looked fantastic.

Sarah . . . dressing for fathers . . . Brickman. Was that the connection? Brickman the father figure who makes the boo-boo go away? Daddy Feel-Good, who in the image of power and kindness, of Dr. Kildare as God the beneficent, suddenly rises in black cape, pointy ears, and bloodshot eyes, raising a surgical knife that suddenly resembles a three-pronged spear?

"James?" Sarah stood above me. "Let me through."

I moved my knees as she squeezed past and sat. I looked at her lovely profile and thought of Brickman slapping it.

We listened to Haydn's Surprise Symphony.

The Surprise Symphony was . . . what can I tell you? Surprising. For those who don't know, the musicians, one by one, fold up their music and leave the stage. Just like that. If you don't read the program notes, as I didn't, it's bizarre.

Afterward Sarah and I walked arm and arm past the fountain. More surprises. Above were a half dozen visible stars. "Enjoy it?" I asked.

"I enjoy you."

"I didn't know Haydn got you so romantic."

"Not Haydn, silly."

She was going to start again with my new purposeful, dangerous, ravishing aura. I hate to take advantage of what might seem like false pretenses, but what the hell. At the very least it was distracting her from tuning in to my less than risk-free existence.

And it was an exceptionally nice change to our relationship. The last two months had been spent on separate sides of the bed. "My place or yours?" I asked, knowing the answer. There's a third part to our equation. "Sarah, what if you found I was doing—"

"What?"

"Something . . . not up-and-up?"

"What?" She stopped walking and stared. "What are you doing, James?"

"Just if. Just if." That's where honesty gets you. "Sarah, look, how long have you known me?"

"Nine months. Tonight," she said. Suddenly she pulled me by the arm. "Come on."

"What?"

"Let's get a cab. I think you've drugged me."

"Drugged?"

"Aphrodisiac." She pulled me down the marble stairs leading to Ninth Avenue. We hailed a cab, got in the door, and gave directions. "Oh, I can't stand it, it's like madness," she hissed, as with a jolt we fell against the backseat. "Watch it, here comes lipstick," she cried, and suddenly was on me.

And all that effect, that planning, dressing, toiletries, worry, and rouge, the practiced centuries of artifice, disappeared in a jumbled, crinkling, panting mass.

Tough, purposeful, and risky it is.

CHAPTER
18

The next morning I got up early. I had work to do.

Keri was bouncing around and promptly attacked when I entered the Kitchen Area. "What were you and Mommy doing last night?"

"Huh?"

"You were making noises. I heard you."

I stared at the little banshee, but the question was heart-achingly sincere. Sarah, apparently enthralled with my sense of "purpose," had moaned and groaned in approval much of last night. I wondered exactly what Keri had heard. "Singing," I said.

"Huh?"

"We were singing. Only you won't know the

song because it's by Haydn. A distant cousin of Michael Jackson."

"Oh," Keri said, stared some more, and finally nodded. To a six-year-old, singing together in bed made perfect sense. "I guess Mommy likes you" she said, matter-of-factly. "Though Mommy likes me more."

"She loves you, Keri."

"I love her too." Keri smiled and nodded at this certainty. Then she seemed to think a moment. "Jamey?"

"What?"

"Are you doing something scary?"

"What do you mean?"

"Mommy worries."

Oh, boy. Were there genes of sensitivity, passed down from mother to child? "Does she say that, honey?" I asked.

"No."

I stared at Keri. A look of wisdom graced her lovely little face.

"Then how do you know she worries?" I asked.

"I know," Keri said, nodding grimly. She looked at me, shrugged, then went bouncing back to whatever else she was doing before my entry into her consciousness.

Was this childlike intuition? The god of guilt, disguised, come to make me feel like a jerk?

I hadn't time for these questions. I needed to get back to my office and look at those procedures, a desire motivated by an imagined or perceived observation made outside the loft last night.

Exiting from the cab, I had noticed someone watching.

Yes, the more arduously I pursued Brickman, the more each shadow and sound began embodying the man's revenge. I'm not used to passionate obsession, and obviously I was obsessed here by the probability of his guilt. Plus I hated the man.

Why? I didn't know why.

But I had a feeling he knew I hated him. And knew I was after him, not just for a lawsuit. His wife, Julie, must have told him about my interest in a clipping in the *Boston Herald* and in his company, Healers Inc. Hell, I'd told her he'd murdered Mindy Sayles. She must have told him that too.

Or no one watched last night. Fine. Dr. Paranoia.

Nonetheless I took a cab on a circuitous route to my office.

Inside I turned on the computer, checked my E-mail, and dusted briefly with an ostrich feather duster, a present from Sarah. Move that dust around. I unwrapped a fresh, crusty croissant and opened a paper cup of coffee from the Lebanese across the street, dunked the croissant into the creamy java—best chemical reaction in the world, croissant corroding into coffee gook—and shuffled through the sheaf of procedures Buzz had handed me last night.

I was trying to find if Brickman had performed

an excess of biopsies in the last four years, which was, as I thought of it, the original reason Mindy had contacted me. I had various numbers corresponding to the various women's ages, and enough numbers in these files of surgical procedures, with patients' names whited out, to give me a decent confidence level (a confidence level means you're confident of your numbers a certain percentage of the time). So all I had to do was sift through, plug all into a spreadsheet, and let Mad Max have a party.

About two hours later I had my numbers double-checked and in. I pressed "calculate," and ten seconds later after lots of number crunching—what is the sound of a number crunched?—the answer arrived.

His invasive procedures were just about average.

I double-checked my figures. I went over each number again. I restarted the process.

Same result.

The croissant and coffee, the remaining crumbs and drips of it, looked toxic. Sarah's feather duster metamorphosed into a voodoo fetish. The guy was clean. Shit.

I shut off the computer.

I looked around my office. It seemed emblematic of my situation. Lobster trap. Roach Motel. Dead end.

Of course I had kind of expected this. I should take this like a risk theorist who weekly repeats in his own column that if you bet against the odds, you'll probably lose. Or if something smells like a rose, chances are it's not a stinkweed.

For consolation I stared at my fault tree.

I now had three murders: Mindy Sayles, Dave Washburn, and Andy Picard. Had the same person killed all three? Were there three different murderers?

I wrote ONE MURDERER, then THREE MURDERERS. Three murderers seemed unlikely. The person who had murdered Washburn had probably murdered Andy Picard too.

I wrote, BRICKMAN COMMITS THE MURDERS HIMSELF.

That seemed wildly improbable. First, Brickman had an alibi for the time of Mindy's death. His office manager swore he was there. Yes, that alibi could be fraudulent, and more checking could prove that, but the odds seemed small.

Another improbability? Though Brickman certainly had a temper, he was by nature and profession a healer, having spent the last twenty years saving lives. To picture his blue-veined surgeon's fingers steering a cab into Mindy Sayles or blowing away Andy Picard seemed unlikely, to put it mildly.

Unless Dr. Brickman was Mr. Hyde.

I wrote SPLIT PERSONALITY on my blackboard. I had a feeling I was exiting reality in a hurry, writing that.

Information. I needed more information.

Hadn't I told Grimes I'd be at the Public Library on Fifth Avenue at 11:00 A.M.? Yes, I had. It was 10:20. Would Grimes show? I'd bet against it.

But I'd bet big time I'd be there.

When was the last time you went? Not just you, New Yorkers, though shame on you if it's been a while, but out-of-towners, tourists, business folks. The flagship of the New York Public Library on Fifth Avenue and Forty-second Street, the largest public library in the world, situated in the midst of Molech, avarice, world angst, and dirty sex, is a living, breathing monument to the human brain.

Plus it's gorgeous. They cleaned up the marble and restored the original murals so it's like a museum where you're allowed to touch the art. The periodicals room, the science and technology division . . . I can spend hours there feeling free of dehumanizing, uncivilizing risks.

So it was slightly disappointing to find, in the Main Reading Room with its fifty-foot-high ceilings and endless rows of studious eggheads, one Lieutenant Grimes seated at a long table, his raincoat rumpled, a scarf concealing his scowl, and looking as if he'd been dragged here against Godzilla's will.

"Good morning," I said.

"There's a half hour wait for the microfilm," he spit out. No "hello" or "¿Qué pasa?" "It's my day off," he hastened to remind me.

"Shush," hissed four others sharing his long table.

"Let's get a viewer," I said, ushering him away from our hecklers. Was this a fish out of water? "A half hour goes quickly," I said.

"Not in this morgue," he groaned.

Beauty is to the beholder.

We found an entire row of empty microfilm viewers and camped out.

"I hate when people say shush." He continued miserably. "Reminds me of school."

"Pipe down," someone said in the row ahead of us.

I checked on the microfilm lady. She shook her head. I turned and oh so slowly retraced my steps.

Well, what could I do in library purgatory? I couldn't talk. Grimes couldn't gripe or scream. I counted books. Grimes practiced clenching his fists.

I finally retrieved the microfilmed April and May *Boston Herald*s from 1964. I spooled them into the viewer, and we both inspected April 1, 1964.

April Fools.

Thirty years ago LBJ was ready for a fateful election, President Kennedy was six months beneath the cold ground of Arlington Cemetery, and what we know as the sixties were ready to roar. Fresh chickens were 29 cents a pound, a fifth of Four Roses $4.95, and a house in Wellfleet seventeen grand. (Seventeen grand? Ah, hindsight.) The Celtics were winning the play-offs, *Bonanza* was on the tube (still is), and *Seven Days in May* was in the movie theaters.

But Thomas Brickman had not made the news. Not even an hour later, when we hit May 1.

"Man, what are you writing?" Grimes asked.

I'd been jotting down the violent crimes I'd come across. Five beatings, three murders, and two rapes. That was for a month. Things since then, if you haven't noticed, have gotten a whole lot more violent. "Know something?" I said. "What was the day Mindy died?"

"Monday."

"The date."

"What the fuck, do I look like a calendar?"

"Today's the ninth," I said, ignoring the man's inner turmoil. "Fourth. April fourth."

I spooled backward. On April 4 thirty years ago the world was mourning General MacArthur. Like all good soldiers, he hadn't died but simply faded away.

There were lots of tributes for the General. And the mention of one rape.

"What were Mindy's sculptures in her loft titled?" I asked Grimes.

"That metal stuff?" Grimes stared at his hands. "Rape. Something to do with rape."

I pointed to the viewer.

BOSTON WOMAN RAPED

April 4—Last night Hannah McCory was

172

raped and beaten to an inch of her life on M
Street by, it is alleged, Barry Tenefly, 25, of
Buzzards Bay. Police today were still seeking
Tenefly, a premed student at Boston College.

Premed?

"They printed the victims' names in those
days," I said.

"So?" Grimes said.

"Shush!" a guy on the other side of the viewer
hissed.

"Lieutenant, what if you just fire off a shot, clip
this guy's dick off?" I said loud enough to be heard
in the next row. A moment of silence was followed
by shuffling footsteps, a coat being grabbed, and
shoes and legs hurriedly moving away.

Grimes grinned. "Best thing you've done yet."

I shrugged, then pointed at the clipping. "Lieutenant, the man who did this was twenty-five.
Twenty-five plus thirty is fifty-five."

Grimes stared.

"Fifty-five is Brickman's age. It's perfect."
Grimes looked as I'd just informed him I was the
wicked witch about to wave my magic froggy.
"True, it's circumstantial. Coincidental. When did
he have a trial?" I scrolled ahead. "We could call
the *Herald*, but it's out of business. Don't the police keep records of this stuff?"

"Man, what are you saying?"

"If Tenefly got convicted, wouldn't he have a
record? Lieutenant, I just want you to make a

phone call. Here's a quarter." I dug in my pocket. Grimes wasn't amused. "Lieutenant, this guy's record is somewhere on file, and you can get ahold of it."

"I don't need a quarter, James. I need to figure out what to say when my buddies at the precinct all together laugh their asses off."

I scrolled to another column.

RAPIST NABBED

April 10—Barry Tenefly was arrested without a struggle last night by the Buzzards Bay Police for the vicious assault and rape of Hannah McCory. He was arraigned today.

Mr. Tenefly was captured in the basement of the home of his father, Victor Tenefly, the owner of a lumberyard. A probable cause hearing has been set.

I scrolled a few days forward. Barry Tenefly was indicted. A trial date was set for July 12 at the Suffolk County Superior Court. "We need another spool," I said.

"What for?"

"To see what happened at the trial. This may be the guy we're looking for."

"We've got to wait another half hour?" Grimes said with a groan.

"So what? What's a half hour? Call and find him."

"This is a fucked-up search for nothing, James."

I unspun the spool and stuck it in its little carton.

"You're the odds man. What are the odds this is the guy? One in a thousand?"

A whole lot worse, I wanted to say but kept my mouth shut. I started toward the microform desk.

"I've got to call Boston," Grimes said with a moan. "No docket number, thirty years ago. Where's your quarter?"

"Use your own," I said, and turned toward the microform desk.

There was a line for microform. I inserted myself ahead of it. "This is a police investigation," I told the woman behind the desk. "Could you please speed up the retrieval?"

If I'd said, "This is a Howdy Dowdy investigation and I'm Uncle Bob," I'd probably have gotten a more sympathetic response. "Half hour is the usual wait," the clerk spit out.

Maybe if I showed her my Nobel Prize.

The microfilm arrived in ten minutes. I felt like slipping the clerk a ten-spot. I ordered three more months of *Herald*s and took July back to the viewer, where I read about the trial. And, reading, got sick.

In 1964 the women's movement, indeed the average female's hope of sexual freedom, despite the pill and free love, was a farfetched dream. A perverted dream, according to most.

Rape? In this Stone Age of women's rights, past sexual history was luridly admissible. Did the victim wear a short skirt? Don't blame a bull for charging a cape.

Three other men at the bar where Tenefly met Hannah—Tenefly and McCory had had three previous dates—stated she was "hot to trot." That, according to the defense, proved beyond reasonable doubt that Hannah was a wanton hussy brazenly inviting unwanted sexual advances.

The judge agreed. For repeatedly raping and beating Hannah McCory, Barry Tenefly received a two-year sentence, which was promptly suspended.

Justice. Thirty years ago.

"Guess what?" Grimes said.

I looked up. He'd been gone twenty minutes.

"I called," he said, sitting beside me. "Want the good news?"

I nodded.

"He's got a record."

"I know."

"You do?"

"I found the trial," I said.

"Then you know more than I do."

I stared at Grimes.

"His records are sealed," Grimes said.

"Sealed?"

"Gone. Erased. Like he never did the crime."

"What do you mean?"

"Judge can do that for a first offense. Ten years later, if he's a good boy, the records are sealed."

I looked at Grimes. "You mean, there's no way to get the records?"

"Not legally."

"What do you mean, not legally?"

"Okay, I got a friend in Boston, in the commissioner's office, owes me a couple favors, I ask him right, we might . . ."

"What?"

"Get the record of his probation officer."

"Fingerprints?"

Grimes stared at me. "Maybe."

"Great!" The tape unwrapped off the spool. I stuck it in its box. No sense spooling through the rest of the *Herald*s.

"James, finding it won't mean shit. The record is inadmissible in court. Inadmissible, you hear? The crime's expunged. Besides, you're just guessing it's Brickman."

"It's the right guess," I said, standing to return to the microform desk. "It's the only guess that makes sense."

A male librarian prissily walked up to us. "You mustn't talk here. There have been complaints."

"Doesn't make sense to me," Grimes said.

"You can't talk," the librarian repeated with a whine.

Grimes turned to me, his face full of blame, then took out his badge and waved it in front of the guy. "You still can't talk, so there," the librarian said with a smirk. Grimes glared. The man turned, clicked his heels, and left. Grimes almost jumped after him.

"Lieutenant . . ."

"Fuck him, fuck you . . . I'm out of here!"

Leaving the Reading Room, passing Mr. Prissy, Grimes whistled, stamped loudly, and winked—politically incorrect yet, I admit, kind of funny.

We walked to the Sixth Avenue exit and descended into the IND. Grimes was taking the subway home to Brooklyn. He waved his badge at the token attendant. "Boy, will I feel safe riding with you," I said.

"No, you won't. You take your own train, James. You've ruined my Saturday."

"Lieutenant, we've got a lot more information. More information is good."

"This is according to your risk theory?"

"The more information," I said, bludgeoning forward, "the more variables. The more variables, the closer we can get to finding the truth. Lieutenant, Brickman is about to do a huge stock deal. He knows a recently murdered patient, and all along he's a past felon."

"We don't know he's a felon," Grimes snapped.

"It ups the probability."

"Probability?"

"That he's involved."

"You're taking the D train?" Grimes said. "You're taking the D?"

I nodded.

"I'm taking the F."

"Lieutenant." I felt like Sisyphus, pushing Grimes up an incline. "You know game theory?" An F train roared around the bend. "I can take the F too," I shouted.

Grimes snapped to attention. "No, you can't."

"What do you mean?"

"You can't. Can't! Can't!" The train stopped and the doors opened. Grimes moved into an open doorway, blocking my way. "New ordinance. New fucking law." I tried to enter alongside him. He pulled out his pistol. "You take this train, you're under arrest. Understand? Under arrest!"

I stared. The man had lost it. Risk theory had curdled his brain. The doors slid in front of him as he waved his pistol. The train started with a lurch.

Inside, Grimes, still gripping the pistol, turned to face a homeless man about to jive him for a quarter.

The homeless guy thought better of that.

CHAPTER
19

I got off the D at the Waverly Theatre and slowly walked down Bleecker. Crossing Sixth, I watched a cardboard carton bounce in front of me, hurled by the wind. Traffic lights swung overhead.

Wind? Who noticed wind? An enormous puzzle was getting pieced together in my head. To supply the several dozen missing pieces, I summoned up my knowledge of game theory.

Game theory—what I mentioned to Grimes and will take just a second to explain—is not an arcane philosophy or the title of a psychological best-seller, but this century's most brilliant mathematical concoction. An offshoot of risk theory, it's used in all sorts of things, including strategies for waging nuclear war.

Here's an example of how it works. In baseball, where the ball gets from the mound to the plate in less than half a second, a hitter must guess at the kind of pitch he's going to see, curve, change-up, fastball, to have any chance of hitting it.

How does he guess? By guessing what his opponent, the pitcher, guesses he's guessing.

That may sound convoluted, but it's nothing more than altering strategy to changing conditions. (The pitcher thinks, *What's the batter expecting? I'll throw what he's not expecting.*)

In short, in game theory, strategy shifts according to your opponent's strategy. And what you think your opponent's strategy is.

Well, if Brickman was after me, his strategy would shift according to what he thought I was thinking.

So what did he think I was thinking?

Brickman knew I was after a clipping. If I could assume the clipping I'd found was the correct one, a large assumption, it led, according to Grimes, to a very dead end. It revealed a thirty-year-old felony that was sealed, which the public, even the law, no longer had access to. It was possible the SEC couldn't even legally stick this fact on a prospectus, even if it knew about it, which it probably didn't.

It wasn't this felony. Couldn't be.

Forget what Brickman thought. How could I get him to think I knew more than I did? If he thought that, he might change his strategy and come after me, as I imagined he had with Mindy, Washburn, and Andy.

Why didn't I fancy that idea?

Turning toward my office, getting smacked in the face by a blast of wind, I decided to appease my growling innards with a snack. I crossed the street to the Lebanese.

I noticed someone behind me, watching. And it wasn't a lonely guy stumbling from a gay bar on the prowl. I know that kind of watching. Living on Christopher Street, the major cruising block of the gay universe, I'm an expert on that kind of watching. This watching wasn't amorous in the least.

I stepped into the grocery store. Hakim, as usual, sat behind the counter, yakking on the phone. "Hakim, listen," I said. "Don't hang up. Don't stop talking. Don't even look at me."

"What?" Hakim said, eyes opening wide.

"Is someone following me? Outside, looking in?"

Hakim smiled at me with his lips, but his eyes nervously glanced at the window and beyond for a few seconds. Then back. "Someone out there," Hakim said, still smiling.

"Can you describe him?"

"Mustache, sunglasses, French hat."

"You mean beret?"

"Yes." Hakim's eyes glanced back into the street, back at me, back at the street. "Gone now," he said.

I walked toward the door. Hakim seemed bewildered. "I'll see you some other time, to explain," I said in what I realized later was a large spurt of optimism.

I walked out into the wind.

Okay, here was the perfect opportunity to get to know more than I did, to supply several missing pieces to my puzzle.

It was also the perfect opportunity to get my head kicked in.

Faced with this choice, I quickly balanced risks against rewards (quickly, as I was being tailed by a potential maniac). Learning more about Mindy's death would hardly equal getting my head kicked in. But my risk of not solving the case and failing at my private detecting fantasy would be, well, almost as awful.

I walked past the Christopher Street Hotel by the West Side Highway. I didn't look back. I knew I was being followed.

Before the light changed, I sprinted against traffic toward the forlorn and now empty semblance of a park by the Hudson River.

I turned and stared back. Across the highway my pursuer seemed confused and about to give up the chase. I reprimanded myself for allowing this possibility when, with a break in traffic, he jumped past a rent-a-truck on his way toward me.

What should I do, turn and use tai chi? My powers of rhetoric? Silence and cunning?

I heard a firecracker.

By the deteriorating piers that stretch like

plowed rows into the Hudson, piers that years ago docked great sailing vessels but now rot in the sun and salt, seeing no greater commerce than dog walks, cruising grounds, and sight-seeing, lots of people pointed. And shouted, "Watch it! Watch it!"

Watch what?

Something whizzed past my ear.

I was being shot at!

Obviously my pursuer's rewards of dropping me with a bullet were far greater than his fears of growing old in Sing Sing.

So I ran like mad.

I had a choice between racing down the pier or continuing to the end of this cul-de-sac, then hurtling over the barrier on the highway toward Bank Street and all the lovely little alleys offering perfect cover for a pistol-wielding killer. I chose the pier. If he followed me to the end, I'd jump into the Hudson. I'd probably get a dose of typhoid from swallowing the river's dirty, polluted water, but hospitals have inoculations, detoxification serums, stomach pumps to counter that. Whereas the medical cure for a bullet to the brain is still on the drawing board.

"He's got a gun!" someone shouted as I raced past. My feet thumped on the wooden planks lining the pier. Where were the police? I had voted for putting more of them on the streets. Of the twenty-four thousand New York City cops, all I needed were a couple!

The wind whipped past my ears, my ragged

breath pounded in my head . . . and I didn't hear him. I didn't hear him!

I turned. He was kneeling, taking aim! I dove and rolled onto the pier as another shot cracked, and a splinter of wood exploded beside me. Something dug into my cheek. I rolled again, then got up in a crouch and zigzagged toward the Statue of Liberty in the distance, a monument to liberty, but not mine, not now. My liberty lay in the puke-green waters of the Hudson.

And then he ran away.

Some people by the pier shouted, but no one chased him. They just watched. I panted like a bellows, my chest on fire. "Run, you fucker, run!" I cried, but it came out a rasp. I shook my fist. I pressed it against my heart.

Half a dozen young men, all prone on the pier, stared up in terror. "What was that?" one squeaked.

Whatever or whoever that was now ran toward the highway, wove through traffic, and disappeared down a side street.

After pulling out a tiny sliver of wood from my cheek, I walked down the pier. I felt like Clint Eastwood after some terrible shoot-out, shuffling past the townsfolk who stare in frightened awe.

A patrol car, red light flashing, pulled up to that semblance of a park, followed by a police scooter. The police scooter sped toward me. "You all right?" the cop cried.

I nodded, still walking.

THE RISK OF MURDER

"Could you stop a second? We want to ask some questions."

Another cop came running up. "What happened?" he said.

"No idea," I said.

"You just taking a walk?"

"Lovely day for it," I said as the wind blew last week's newspapers into our faces.

Cop cars from all over the city were arriving. It looked like a regular convention. Make sure to close the stable door after the horse escapes, boys!

I got whisked to the Sixth Precinct. It was lots of fun riding in a squad car, something I've longed to do since I was a wee tyke.

Upstairs at the precinct I met several very nice police officers, including one Lieutenant Lowery. That sounded familiar.

"Do I know Lieutenant Grimes?" he asked like a psychotherapist, answering a question with a question. "Wait a second, you're . . . Dr. Risky, right?"

"Something like that," I muttered.

After listening a little to my story, Lowery picked up his phone and tapped out the number for Grimes's beeper. "Send a squad car to pick Grimes up," Lowery shouted across the room.

"Oh, no, I don't think so," I said.

"You don't think so?" Lowery stared at me as if I'd just appeared in my seat.

"It's his day off."

"It's his case. He'll work it."

I shook my head. I had to get out of here. "Lieutenant, why don't you just talk to him on the phone?"

"He gets OT coming down. You," he said, staring at me, "need protection. Someone to watch your place."

I said that'd be fine and gave Lowery Sarah's address, saying I'd been followed there too.

"How come you won't wait for Grimes?" Lowery asked.

Because if Grimes saw me again today, he'd shoot me, I didn't say.

A pretty Hispanic lady cop walked over. "Take this guy to Christopher Street and make sure he gets in his office in one piece," Lowery said. The woman stared back. "Someone just tried to shoot him. It's Grimes's case."

"Oh, Grimes," the woman said, as if that explained everything. I read her name tag: Rosie Morales. She was awfully small, minuscule actually. "So, Mr. . . ."

"Risky," Lowery said.

"Denny," I said. "James."

"Mr. Denny, then," she said, and I followed her out the office and down the stairs.

In the waning sunlight on Bleecker Street Rosie inspected the boo-boo on my cheek. "Think I need stitches?" I asked.

Rosie shook her head and smiled. "I'll wait till

you open the shades if everything's all right," she said.

And if it wasn't, Rosie Morales would doubtless hurl her little body against my door, break through, and disarm my six-foot-two pursuer.

Inside was a message from Sarah. Did we have a date tonight? I closed the lights, double-locked the office, and took the elevator up to my fifth-floor apartment.

And looked at my face in the mirror. First a shaving accident, and now . . . shaving with a semiautomatic? The cut was a puncture, not wide but deep. It wouldn't leave a scar. My motion-picture career was intact.

I put hydrogen peroxide on it, then turned on the shower to steamy and pulled off my clothes. Curiously I inspected my underpants. No telltale stains of fouling myself in fear. My tough guy certificate was in the mail! Second thought, maybe this was the foolscap itself, a pair of unstained Jockey shorts.

I spent about twenty minutes scrubbing myself down, inhaling the steam, trying to relax. I'd double-locked my door, and my windows have gates, but every noise in the building, every squeak of the pipes or slamming of a neighborly door, brought hackles to the back of my neck. Living a life of fear would take some getting used to.

I'd shifted gears from superfast to warp speed on the highway toward risk. Risk assessing had skipped risk taking to become risk engorging.

Where would it end? Would I soon face that ultimate risk, utter and irrevocable loss of life expectancy?

I called Sarah and got her machine. I wanted to tell her to move to her mom's for a day or two but didn't know how to do that in a message without alarming her like mad. Maybe Lowery would send a cop down. Maybe he'd send Rosie Morales. Maybe Rosie and Sarah would have tea.

I got dressed and packed a bag. Nothing elaborate, a tie and jacket and a change of underwear, just in case I couldn't repeat my command performance when confronting major fear. I took five of the hundreds I had lying around, walked out, and peered down the hallway. No bullets whizzed past my head. I double-locked my door, took the elevator down, and walked out into the early Saturday evening crowd. No cabs tried to run me over.

I stepped into the street and hailed one. Inside the hack a Chinese cabbie turned and said, "Yes?" or "¿Sí?" or "Huh?" One of those.

"La Guardia Airport," I said. "The Shuttle."

The cabbie stared at me for a prescient moment, then nodded knowingly. Had he a clue what I'd said? He stepped on it, though. I fell back in the seat.

When a man attacks your home turf, an old Taoist proverb says, "Go attack his."

Boston, here I came.

CHAPTER
20

At nine o'clock at Logan Airport eight rental car agencies stared hungrily as I walked among them. "Yes, Mr. Denny, yes, sir," they said. Finally I chose one and received not only a car but a map detailing my precise route to my reserved hearth, home, and hotel. And then a carport, and a magnetic card for my room, in which I found a little refrigerator filled with all sorts of goodies, juices, and candy bars.

I quickly ate two chocolate bars, one after another, like a little kid. Why? I wanted to feel like a little kid, a little kid who's safe, happy, and warm.

I had been searching for that feeling when I made my cabbie get off the highway twice on the way to the airport, and I'd found it when no one

191

followed us onto the off or on ramp. The feeling persisted when no one pursued me onto the plane or shadowed me at Logan.

I had a third candy bar in celebration.

I descended in the elevator to the hotel lounge, which looked like a gold lamé planetarium, and had a couple of Heinekens while watching a guy and girl sing old Carpenter songs. Ravenous even after all that chocolate, I ordered a hamburger platter. The girl sang old Judy Collins songs. I finished and, instead of paying with dirty cash, signed for it with a John Hancock flourish, for which I received another "Yes, Mr. Denny."

I raced back up to my room and slept like the dead.

At nine the next morning back in the lounge, I poured a cup of self-serve, milk, sugar, dropped my seventy-five cents in a metal container, and walked to a bank of public phones.

The magic card fantasy was, of course, just that. All these joyous services eventually were coming out of my pocket. So instead of incurring the fifty-cent surcharge on each phone call made from my room, I metamorphosed a phone booth, a stack of quarters, and my styrofoam cup of steamy joe into an office away from home.

A half hour later this transformed risk assessor was on his way. The snazzy sports coup they'd upgraded me to, when the promised plain Jane wasn't in the lot, transported me speedily onto the interstate. Under New England skies, leaning back in a racer's bucket seat, listening to the cool boom of fusion jazz, I experienced the birthright of every American who doesn't live in New York City: the chance to steer a ton and a half of steel wherever the hell you like. Guaranteed by our Constitution.

I wasn't thinking of the angry messages I'd just listened to. Sarah, upset at my breaking our little get-together last night, wanted a detailed explanation. Grimes, screaming how his day off was ruined twice, swore he'd train his kid to become a Ninja to take revenge.

Instead I took in the rolling clouds and the winding road, in my wheels, with my sounds, and no one following me. Despite the chances of traffic fatality, I hadn't felt as risk-free in a week.

I drove past Plymouth and its famous rock toward the Cape, an hour drive. Down the Cape Cod Canal, under the Bourne Bridge, I made a right around a rotary into Buzzards Bay.

I'd checked the phone directory. No Victor Tenefly. No Tenefly, period. Beyond that I hadn't a clue whom to ask about a thirty-year-old lumberyard.

Besides, it was Sunday, so everything municipal was locked up tight. I drove down the main strip, wondering what inspiration would fall directly on my head.

It turned out to be a synagogue.

Brickman was Jewish. At least he'd received

awards from B'nai B'rith. Tenefly was a Jewish name, wasn't it?

Here in plain sight was a temple.

I parked and walked in. Should I wear a yarmulke? A religious class was taking place in one of the rooms. Beyond that in an administrative room, and yes, on Sunday, not at all the Jewish day of rest, a dark-haired young woman was working. I told her I had to inform Victor Tenefly of a windfall inheritance. Did she know his whereabouts?

She pored through a bunch of thick administrative books. Nothing. Was anyone here older than twenty-three? "Mr. Nussbaum," she said. He lived three houses up and had been praying here and at the old temple for fifty years. She warned me he didn't hear well. He was in his eighties.

"Mr. Nussbaum," I cried, knocking on the door of a house set back from the road. After a long wait I shouted and pounded again, and after a longer wait an old man opened the screen door. I explained who I was, why I was here, in fact everything you'd want to know if you weren't interested in the truth.

"Money, you say?" I think that was the only word Mr. Nussbaum caught.

"Well, I'm not at liberty to disclose the amount Tenefly inherited, but it's not chicken feed. Did you know Victor Tenefly personally?" I asked. "He had a lumberyard."

"What'd you say?" Mr. Nussbaum muttered, turning his mottled ear toward me.

"Lumberyard! What happened to it?" I shouted.

"What?" Mr. Nussbaum said.

"To the lumberyard!" This was fun, tearing information from a soundproofed skull.

"Sold it. He's dead."

"Shit," I said. Nussbaum didn't hear that either. "What about his son? Barry?"

"What?"

I took a deep breath, smiled grandly at the old man, whose expression of bewildered concern hadn't altered a jot since he'd come to the door, and repeated the question directly into his ear canal.

And finally I learned that Victor's son, Barry, had got into some kind of trouble with a girl, and there'd been a trial, and Victor had borrowed lots of money for a lawyer and finally sold the yard to pay off debts.

"Then what happened? To his son."

Nussbaum said he went away. Didn't know where.

"What about the mother?"

"What?"

Shouting "mother" on Sunday was probably a crime in Buzzards Bay, but I took the risk.

The mother died young, Nussbaum said. "He was a nice boy," he added. The definition of "nice" would be terrifically updated if I told Nussbaum who Barry Tenefly really was.

Beyond this, Nussbaum had little to add. This,

not at all oddly, made me very depressed. Flying to Boston and driving here for no good reason whatever kind of dampened my Sunday spirits.

Plus it started to rain.

"Shit!" I cried at the now-noxious sounds of Kenny G filling the car. I drove back to Boston.

I did get the phone number of Tina Nussbaum, Nussbaum's sixty-year-old daughter, who had personally known Barry. She'd be in tomorrow.

So for the moment the newspaper article from thirty years ago was all I had to catch Brickman. It now lay in my lap, and it said M Street. I'd already tried the phone book for a listing of Hannah McCory on M Street or anywhere else. Nothing.

Barry Tenefly had, for the moment, escaped my risk-assessing fingers. Finding Hannah might lead me to him.

A map, care of the hotel, directed me toward a seedy area in South Boston with lots of old gas guzzlers in the streets. All the buildings needed a fresh sandblasting and a coat of paint. Some needed a fresh dynamiting.

The precinct here might have records of the case.

Squad cars in front of a large turn-of-the-century building proclaimed its purpose. I parked and raced through the rain.

The desk sergeant looked like a character out of Dick Tracy, nose and chin sharpened two-dimensionally. Several old lamps bathed everything in the green glow of an institutional time warp. "An address you're looking for?" the sergeant said with a slight brogue.

"Something like that," I said. At least I wasn't shouting.

"But the records are centralized nowadays," the sergeant said. "Go to City Hall."

"It's Sunday."

"That it is."

"Can I get the address of someone now?"

"Ah," said the sergeant. "And have you tried the phone book?"

Had I tried the phone book. "I mean like a search of motor vehicle licenses. Do you have access?"

"That we do. Twenty-four hours."

"Could you do a search for a Hannah McCory?"

"And whom may I say requests it?"

Dr. Risk wasn't a household name in Beantown. "The New York City Police?" I said.

"Well, that might get some action now. Do you perhaps have identification?"

"I could have someone call you."

"Could you now?"

What an agreeable manner! I wondered how long it would take me to vault up over the desk and choke the agreeable life right out of the man. "Look, is there a Catholic church in the neighborhood?"

"Is there? What do they say, is there a pope in the woods?"

I stared at the sergeant. "Bear in the woods," I said. "It's a bear in the woods."

"Is it now?"

I walked to the door, impatient to get out before I committed a crime.

I did find one church two blocks away called Our Blessed Sacrament. Our Blessed Sacrament was like a security computer; I lacked the right password. Each great, carved, oaken, and thoroughly locked entrance kept me from prayer, confession, salvation, and the church register, where I hoped to find the baptism, communion, and marriage of Hannah McCory. Of course I hadn't a clue if Hannah had ever set foot in this church or any other.

I didn't particularly want to spend another night in Beantown, but when I finally got through the door, the one priest not involved with mass told me that the register, locked in the rectory across the way, was accessible only by a nun who wasn't in on Sundays.

So I found a nearby hotel, considerably less expensive, where everyone didn't say, "Yes, sir," and "Yes, Mr. Denny." After a matinee movie I bought a paperback, ate dinner at an Arby's, and returned in the rain. The clerk downstairs sold me a pint of Canadian whiskey at a premium. Liquor stores open in Boston on Sunday? Come on.

In my room, with wallpaper peeling and a neon sign not exactly blinking but visible from my hotel window, and a slug of whiskey in a plastic cup, I felt like a real shamus.

CHAPTER
21

At the crack of dawn I had a nightmare. I immediately forgot what it was about but couldn't go back to sleep. I finally dragged myself into the bathroom, turned on the shower, and let the hot water scald me awake.

I dressed and went down the elevator into a still-sleeping city. At a breakfast place I ordered eggs, despite the risks of cholesterol. I was starving. While the order got prepared, I sat at a public phone and called my answering machine.

There was a message from Sarah. We'd been playing phone tag. On my return to New York I'd tell all, I promised myself. Like George Washington and his cherry tree, I'd tell the truth.

My machine had no messages from Grimes.

Nor Buzz. Nor my editor, who calls every other Monday to hear me pitch column ideas. Nor Publishers Clearing House telling me I'd won millions.

Fine with me.

At 8:30 A.M. I walked into the Clerk's Office at City Hall and boldly asked for the voter registration list. And boldly was I shown it. It's public record.

Hannah McCory had not voted for the last three years. To find out she had not voted for the last thirty years would require a written request and a three-week wait.

Why wouldn't she have voted? Was she a bad citizen? Had she moved out of Boston? Had she got married and changed her name? What were the probabilities of these?

I knew the probabilities of getting married. Eighty-six percent of the female population does.

Let's move closer to certainty. What was the highest probability for her not voting?

Being dead.

Yes! She couldn't have voted if she'd passed away (though in some wards in Boston this is no impediment). But more important, there'd be a death certificate. This handy device, along with a birth certificate, gets attached to all of us upon arrival and departure from this organized world of ours, and it contains loads of useful information that risk assessors and actuaries and even ordinary folks can make excellent use of.

Like a last address.

Next door the Department of Public Health contained all the records of births, deaths, and marriages in Massachusetts for the last 150 years. I filled out a form, forked over six dollars, and sat down for a ten-minute wait.

And there it was, delivered to me by a smiling clerk. Hannah had died three years ago, at age forty-eight, from a metastasis of breast cancer.

Breast cancer.

"Can I keep this?" I asked, waving the evidence. The clerk shrugged. Six dollars for a photocopy? Have a party.

I drove to the address on the copy where the super, a large, perspiring Mexican named Fernandez, said, *Sí*, he remembered Hannah McCory. Did anyone come visit? The super shrugged. Anything else you can tell me? Where she went to church?

"Church," Fernandez said, his face brightening. "She love to go to church. My wife go to the same church. Our Blessed Sacrament."

Small world, wasn't it?

I drove back down toward M Street. Hannah McCory hadn't moved around much since 1964.

The rectory was a small building attached to the Gothic structure with the door clearly labeled. I walked inside and met a bright, freshly scrubbed young lady smiling rabidly at me behind a large desk cluttered with old ledgers, dusty tomes, and, of all things, a brand-new computer. "I wonder if you or anyone else," I said, "remember Hannah McCory."

"Hannah McCory, Hannah McCory, Hannah McCory," she repeated like an incantation. "Is she a member of the church?"

"She was. She's dead."

"I'm sorry," the young lady said. No need to be, I might have replied but hadn't time, for she was already asking for the spelling, then hurriedly scanning a directory.

"Perhaps one of the priests . . . " I started to suggest.

"No, no, no, they're not in. Sister Cary! She is. In." She stood, no, leaped up. "Should I knock?" She turned. "I mean, that door. There. Inside."

Well, frenetic church clerk, yes, knock, go ahead. So the young lady knocked three times, three whacks actually, then stuck her head in for some whispering.

I entered the inner sanctum.

Sister Cary sat at an even bigger desk, a medieval-looking desk covered with ancient and possibly valuable books. She wore the long nun's habit plus that square hat or veil covering everything except her rosy face; styles hadn't changed much in the church since the Council of Worms. It was hard to tell her age in all this. Hard to tell gender as she was smoking a small cigar. Hard to tell species. "Good morning, sir," she said, confirming my suspicion she was human. And Irish, for I heard a slight brogue. She took a long puff on her stogy and stared fiercely at me. "And what can I and Christ do for you this lovely day?"

"Well, Sister, I don't know what Christ can do, but maybe you could help me with a matter concerning Hannah McCory," I said, trying to absorb all I saw.

"Hannah McCory, Hannah McCory?" Sister Cary repeated. Had Hannah's name been transformed into song? The sister blew a smoke ring into the air and studied its dissipation. "I knew Hannah. You?"

"Actually no, but I'm trying to reopen a rape case. I don't think justice got served."

"Oh, you don't, do you?" The good sister glared at me. "Well, Mr.—what was your name?"

"Denny," I said.

"You bet your britches it wasn't served. Justice." She glared disdainfully at her stogy, then took another puff. "I never heard anything so awful in my entire life. That the armed, miserable sinner got off scot-free."

"Do you recall the trial, Sister?"

"No. I didn't come to these shores till 1971. But I heard what happened. Disgraceful."

"Did she do anything further about the matter?" I asked.

"Like what? What could she do? Find a gun and shoot the man? I would have done that, found a gun, God forgive me, but, Hannah, bless her soul, was a saint. She lived with the sadness."

"You're saying she forgave her rapist?"

"Good Lord, I hope not," Sister Cary said with a snort.

I could get to like this lady. "Did she ever run into him?"

"Wouldn't think so. Never mentioned it if she did. Kept her grief to herself, poor dear."

"Did she ever marry?"

"Marry?" Sister Cary said, measuring relevance with some religious yardstick.

"I need information about her family. From her family."

"Ah." Sister Cary nodded. "Yes, she married."

"Do you know the date?"

"She married several months after my coming to these shores. I attended the wedding. The exact date's in the register."

"What became of her husband?"

"Husband's dead."

"Would she have any other family I could speak to?"

"She had a daughter."

"Is the daughter"—I hated to ask this; I sounded like a gravedigger—" . . . living?"

"Afraid I couldn't tell you, Mr. Denny. Saw her ten years before. Off to school, I think. A fine and beautiful young woman, full of life."

"Which school, Sister?"

"Now, I couldn't tell you that either. Don't remember these things."

"What did her husband die of?"

"Lung cancer. Smoked like a chimney," Sister Cary said, taking the stogy out of her mouth and with a wicked grin blowing a stream of smoke up toward the painted windows. She had a sense of humor, Sister Cary. "Didn't see the daughter at the funeral."

"Why?" I asked.

"Wasn't her real father." And then Sister Cary's eyes narrowed. "Mr. Denny," she said slyly, "Hannah had her child . . . from a previous . . . " She stared up at the ceiling and smirked.

I suspected she meant Hannah's daughter was illegitimate. "Sister Cary, would she have been baptized here? Can I look at the register?"

Sister Cary ground out her stogy in an ashtray thick with ash—one of a long line of stogies—and said, "That, sir, you cannot. We have a new assistant outside, as no doubt you have seen, and she's deep in the process of computerizing the past hundred and twelve years. I'm afraid you and everyone else will have to wait till she's finished."

"When might that be?"

"God willing, a month."

A month? Brickman's deal would have come and gone. "Is there any way to speed up the process? A donation?"

"Good grief, my boy, are you trying to bribe the Catholic Church?"

I told Sister Cary she could call it what she liked, but I needed the information immediately.

Sister Cary stood. She moved toward me with all that rustling of cloth. It sounded like my hotel curtains. "Mr. Denny, we will gratefully accept your donation, whatever your motive. But there's truly nothing I can do. Perhaps the police . . . " And she gestured me to leave.

I miserably stood. Her cigar smoke hung in the air like a ghost escaped from a nearby crypt.

"If I can think of any other information about Hannah, her child, or Mr. Sayles, I will certainly set it aside and give you a call."

"Fine," I said, handing her my card and turning. And got as far as the door. "What did you say?" I cried, turning back.

"Say, sir?"

"A name! A man's name!"

"Hannah's husband?" Sister Cary said. "Michael . . . Sayles?"

My heart did a stutter step.

"Are you all right, Mr. Denny. You look thunderstruck."

I grabbed Sister Cary and gave her a big kiss on her cheroot-smudged mouth. I heard her shriek as I ran out of the office.

CHAPTER
22

It was the piece of the puzzle that made all else fit!

Mindy was Hannah's daughter!

Hannah must have changed her name back to McCory after her husband's death.

Mindy had mentioned finding the clipping in her mother's apartment. Finding the clipping. It implied Mindy hadn't known about the rape but discovered the awful fact coming across a yellowed newspaper clipping after her mother's death. "Kept her grief to herself, poor dear," Sister Cary had said about Hannah. Probably kept it even from her own daughter.

So what did Mindy do upon finding out? (1) Struggle terribly with the knowledge? (2) Create sculptures about rape to deal with her anger? (3) Stumble upon Brickman and know it was him?

That last part, (3), wasn't clear. Why would she try to sue Brickman if she knew? And again, according to Grimes, the clipping wasn't blackmailing material. It couldn't stop the public offering. It might throw a monkey wrench into Brickman's marriage, if Mindy told his wife, but a look at Julie Brickman's eye kind of indicated Brickman wasn't too worried about that.

Lots of questions but now some answers. If fingerprints verified Brickman as Tenefly, that would stir the interest of Lieutenant Grimes.

The shuttle back to New York was delayed. April showers bring May flowers. April thunderstorms bring transportation nightmares. La Guardia was shut.

While I waited, I made a few phone calls. Finally I got through to Sarah. "Hi," I said, happy to hear her voice.

"James Denny, I hate you."

"Well, I'm glad you got that off your chest," I replied, somewhat wounded. What was going on? Was she miffed I'd canceled our date?

"Nothing's off my chest. Where are you?"

I told her Boston.

"Why didn't you tell me you were going?"

"Leave a message? I hate to tell anything that way."

"But why Boston?"

"Why?" I was telling the truth, like George

Washington. "Business. It was sudden." That was true. "I got a phone call." That wasn't.

"From who?"

"A colleague. I had to look at a dump site." Dump site? My nose grew longer. Well, I couldn't explain on the phone. I'd explain when I got back. "Sarah, it's long distance," I said. "It's costing a fortune."

"It's after five."

I mollified and coddled her and made a kissing sound in the receiver and felt terrible doing all this, but I'd feel more terrible having her scream and hang up on me if I told the truth. I would come clean tomorrow. It's just the timing was awful now.

"I am worried," she said softly. "And not just about you."

"What do you mean?" I heard a long distance sniffle. "Sarah, are you crying?" I didn't know what this was about. "Sarah, please, I miss you." I heard thunder in the background. "Is Keri there?"

"She's having dinner at a friend's."

"Tell her hello from Dr. Risk."

"James, please be safe, will you?"

What was going on? Were we both getting more paranoid by the minute? "I'll see you tomorrow," I said.

"I love you," Sarah said.

I slowly hung up.

Tomorrow. Tomorrow I'd tell her. All would get resolved tomorrow. All the particulars, and she'd be happy and satisfied, seeing I was finally up front, truthful, and honest.

That was the good angel talking. The bad angel said, "If you tell her the truth, dummy, she'll be mad enough to spit. 'Why are you risking your life?' she'll cry. It's dangerous and selfish and childish pretending you're a private eye.'"

Sarah would have to reconcile herself to the new me, the me who took chances, who was now much less afraid of danger. She would have to do so as soon as I reconciled myself to the new me.

I phoned Grimes. He picked up on the first ring. "Where the hell are you, James?"

"Boston, Lieutenant."

"Boston?"

"Lieutenant, I've got very interesting news."

"So do I. We found the driver."

What was *he* talking about?

"Guy that drove the cab, hit Mindy? We found him. Charged him with the murder."

"The hack driver?" I cried. "That's crazy. He didn't do it, Lieutenant. Why would he do it?"

"Because he doesn't know how to drive."

I stared at the receiver. Ask a stupid question, get a stupid answer.

"James, his license has been suspended three times. He hit someone before."

"Lieutenant, what about the guy who tried to shoot me?"

"We're investigating, James. One crime at a time."

"Are you telling me that was a drive-by? A mugging?"

Silence from Grimes.

"What about Washburn? Picard?"

"James, the case is closed."

I stared at the receiver. Case closed? Was this a joke? "Did Brickman make a phone call?" I asked. "Is that what's happening?"

Grimes paused on that. "I'm not even going to answer, James. I'm not even going to imagine you're accusing me or anyone else with that shit. You've seen too many movies."

"I'm not accusing, I just—"

"I don't want to talk to you anymore, okay? I want you back here to ID the cabbie. Pick him out of a lineup. Tomorrow." And he hung up.

I stared at the receiver, then placed it in its cradle and looked around the terminal lobby.

They'd solved the case?

Okay, as far as Grimes was concerned, Barry Tenefly wasn't Thomas Brickman. Even if he was, there was nothing concrete Mindy Sayles could blackmail him with.

But Siravindu Singh the cab driver? And the rest a coincidence? Please!

They herded us onto a plane around ten. The storm was heading toward us, the pilot said over the intercom. "We've got just ten minutes, folks, to get our act in the air."

We waited twenty on the runway.

I started to pray. That may seem hypocritical

for a dyed-in-the-wool risk assessor like myself, to pray against odds (in this case for odds; commercial flights are extremely safe), but risk theorists can believe in divine intervention. It's a way to hedge your bets.

It was also a way to pray for justice. If we crashed, Brickman would go scot-free.

With the wind whipping great sheets of rain against the plastic windows and Walpurgisnacht raging outside, we taxied down the runway. The plane rattled and shook. An overhead compartment popped open, and someone's coat fell into my lap. A woman raised her hands in prayer. I added my silent hosanna: Bring us, dear Lord, beneficent chance.

We were off the ground, climbing through wind shear. Our section cheered.

As we approached La Guardia, the storm vanished and a full moon, out of nowhere, sailed peacefully over Long Island Sound.

Rational risk assessor that I am, I took that as a positive sign.

CHAPTER
23

The cab dropped me off around three in the morning. The rain had scared away tourists and hustlers, so Christopher Street was empty, raising the probability that I wouldn't be followed into my office or have to worry about intruders climbing down the air shaft.

I worried nonetheless.

To get Brickman, I needed real proof. Everything else was smoke and mirrors. Real proof, which I didn't have.

An ingredient was missing.

I turned on the lights in my office and stared at the blackboard. Above the base of my fault tree, which said, MINDY KILLED BY CAB, I had several reasonable routes leading to Brickman, all with a growing probability of success. For instance, above THOMAS BRICKMAN RESPONSIBLE I now wrote BRICKMAN RAPED MINDY'S MOTHER. Mindy knowing that, or Brickman's thinking she knew, could steer the two on a collision course.

But would it cause Brickman to kill her?

Why not simply buy her off? Or dismiss her with Grimes's argument that the records were sealed and the rapist unidentifiable. The fact was neither Mindy nor anyone else could legally uncover Brickman's crime.

But just suppose Brickman didn't know this. Suppose he'd panicked, acted impulsively.

Brickman hadn't gotten where he had in life by impulsiveness, so this was unlikely.

Grimes had the cabdriver, Siravindu Singh, in custody. He would be charged with manslaughter, reckless endangerment, driving without a license, and anything else the police could toss his way. He was headed to prison unless his lawyer could strike a deal. If that deal included Thomas Brickman, I'd be reading about it now in the papers.

Singh hadn't killed Mindy.

I stared at the blackboard. I looked over the numbers, the various dates. There had to be a pattern, a clue missed.

The dates. Mindy was twenty-nine. When was her birthday, hadn't she told me? She said thirty in . . . January? She said January. So? She was a

Capricorn. Or was it Aries? What's the difference? April to January. 4/1 to 1/1 . . .

It hit me! It hit me!

The next thing I knew, it was nine o'clock and the phone was ringing. The answering machine clicked in. Hang-up. I hate those.

I brushed my teeth, showered, and got a cup of coffee down. I picked up the phone and called Brickman's office.

It was time to rumble, as they say.

"Good day," said Julie, office manager supreme, with those clipped British diphthongs, after picking up the phone. "What may I do for you?"

"Mrs. Brickman?" I said. Instant silence on the line. I had played a hunch the office manager providing Brickman's alibi was his wife. Who else would perjure herself and probably receive a black eye for not doing it quickly enough? The British accent? British and Southern accents aren't that dissimilar. Perhaps Julie was honing her acting skills. "Mrs. Brickman," I said, "my name's James Denny. I chased you in the street. I left my card?"

There was a pause. "Mr. Denny, I'm going to hang up on you," Julie Brickman said with a Dallas instead of a London accent.

I clicked the recording button on my answering machine. "Please don't, Mrs. Brickman. I have something very important to tell your husband. It's in your interest too."

"He's a very busy man, Mr. Denny. He's with several patients."

"My information is in reference to incidents in Boston," I said. Did Julie have a clue to Brickman's past? I doubted it. "Please tell him. I'll be waiting," I said, and hung up.

I phoned the Spying Store. I started to ask Richie about the availability of certain items when call waiting beeped in. I put Richie on hold and clicked the other line.

"Mr. Denny," said Thomas Brickman.

"Hold on one second, Doctor." I clicked back to Richie. My heart was pounding. "Richie, I'll call back later."

"Sure thing, Dr. Risk."

I clicked on to Brickman's line. "Dr. Brickman," I said, and took a breath. "Thank you for calling."

"What do you want, Denny?"

No more Mr. Nice Guy. I could live with that. "I thought you'd be interested in information I have about your old stomping grounds. Boston."

There was a pause. "Those are not my old stomping grounds, Denny. And I'm considering this call one more part of a methodical harassment of my wife."

"I didn't beat her up, Brickman."

"I'm counting to three, Denny. Then I'm coming after you with everything I've got. And that's a lot, my friend."

"I found the clipping."

"One . . . two . . ."

"I know who Mindy Sayles really is," I said.

I didn't hear "three."

"Want to talk more?" I asked. I could hear the water dripping in my kitchen sink. "I said, want to talk more, Brickman?"

"Yes, maybe we could do that," Brickman said in a tone quite different from before. "Perhaps we might have . . . something to discuss. My schedule gets lighter . . ."

"I'll see you in an hour, Brickman," I said. "At my office. See you in an hour." And I hung up.

An hour to get ready. That would do. I called Grimes and, after giving my name, was told he was out in the field. Out in the field? What did that mean? Was he at the corner buying Twinkies? "Could you beep him?" I asked the patrolman who'd answered his phone. "I have a very important message."

"What is it?"

"Thomas Brickman will pick me up at eleven. At my place. It's very important he get that."

"He won't get it in an hour. He's on a case."

"This is a case," I said.

"Maybe you want to speak to someone else."

"Okay, let me talk to Lieutenant Lowery."

"Not in."

"Rosie Morales?"

"Nope. Uh, someone's calling me, Mr.—"

"Denny! Didn't you take my name?"

"How you spell that?"

"D-e-n-n-y . . . never mind, never mind." And I hung up.

I called the precinct number and got the day sergeant. I repeated my message. He assured me it'd go out immediately to Lieutenant Grimes. In fact, he assured so many times I didn't believe him.

I didn't have time for this.

I got dressed and went out. Beautiful day, in the sixties, not a cloud in sight. I swore to myself I'd be around later to enjoy it.

I walked quickly toward the Spying Store to buy a tiny voice-activated tape recorder. Just like in the movies, I repeated maniacally to myself, I was going to get Brickman to confess.

"You all right, chief?" Richie said, a little worried when I walked in the door.

"Why?"

"Your shirt's buttoned wrong."

Well, I was in a hurry. I rebuttoned while Richie fetched a new recorder. "Show me how to work this, Richie."

"You want me to strap it on?"

"Make sure to get the chest hairs," I said. A joke. Richie didn't laugh.

"Your hands are shaking," he said.

"Too much coffee." Come on, Dr. Risk, get it together. "And I need one more thing."

Fifteen minutes later I walked back up the

street. The wire was pasted to my chest hairs. My hands had stopped trembling. Everything would be fine.

I unlocked my office and went in. Rosie, the cop, was nowhere in sight. Grimes had undoubtedly called her off. Well, he'd got his murderer—what was his name?—Siravindu. Sounded like a Hindu god. God of life and death. Creator and destroyer? I should know that god's name. I was currently playing footsie with him.

There were no messages. Where was everyone? I started getting angry at Grimes, very angry, and angry at the stupidity of the police and their lack of regard for my health. I even got angry at the mayor's office and the Department of Sanitation.

Of course none of this anger would change the fact that I, single-handedly, had got myself into this mess. I alone had disobeyed common sense and, all by my lonesome, shimmied out onto this limb.

I made one last phone call, to Buzz. Not in. Why didn't I think about these things before calling Brickman? What was my rush? I could have hired my own personal Praetorian Guard before dangling the bait. True, I wasn't sure Brickman would nibble. Nibble? Swallow it hook, line, and sinker.

It was further proof I knew Brickman's motive. Proof I had proof.

A horn honked outside. I peered through the Venetian blinds of my basement window and spotted a tan Mercedes. I took a deep breath, walked out, double-locked my door, and ascended the steps.

Brickman glared at me through his closed, tinted window.

"Nice car," I said, and got in.

CHAPTER
24

Brickman wore a suit and tie that probably cost more than Mindy's retainer. He looked wonderful. I'd have to ask where he shopped.

The car smelled brand-new. There was real leather upholstery. Real snakeskin for Brickman's shoes. Real Irish linen for his shirt. Everything about the man spelled CLASS.

Except this wasn't Thomas Brickman.

"Good morning, Mr. Denny." The "mister" was back. Fear gets you respect.

"And top of the morning to you," I said, my facetiousness trying to mask my fear right now at taking the biggest risk of my life.

Brickman's eyes seemed to bore into mine,

searching for the bones of my motives. "What should we do, Mr. Denny?"

"Oh, I don't know. How about a ride?"

Brickman nodded, depressed the gas, and we were off. He turned right onto the West Side Highway, euphemistically a highway this far downtown despite its traffic lights and crossroads like anywhere else. Beautiful sunlight sparkled on the Hudson. Lighting and coloring by spring. "Nice day for a drive," I said. "Nice car you've got too. I really like the smell of leather."

"Mr. Denny, why did you call me?"

"To get acquainted. At this stage of the game it seemed appropriate, know what I mean?"

Brickman wasn't enjoying our conversation. He frowned and looked right and left. "I was informed your lawyer called mine," he said. "I hate to say this, but I've had only three lawsuits, and all were dismissed. You see, Mr. Denny, I always win."

"This time you won't," I said.

We had been driving north and were now at a light near Forty-second Street. Brickman reached forward and clicked on the radio, which automatically and digitally progressed from station to station. When it paused on Aretha Franklin singing "Pink Cadillac," Brickman punched a button and turned up the sound.

"I didn't know you were a music lover," I said, raising my voice.

Brickman smiled icily. It was the first time I'd

seen him smile, icily or not. "Just in case you're transmitting, Mr. Denny," he said.

The light changed, and we coasted toward the ramp and the real "highway" part at Fifty-seventh Street.

"Transmitting? You mean, you think I'm having us followed?" I said with as much naïveté as I could muster. Me have someone follow you?

Why didn't I?

We drove up the ramp. A cop was helping the mess of converging traffic.

Suddenly I had a feeling my whole plan had run amok. None of it was going to work. I wanted to turn and shout at the traffic cop, "Help! Help me!"

We sped past before I did.

Calm down, James. Down. My plan was risky, but Brickman would show his hand. And the risks, though now much greater than I predicted, would diminish in the face of the rewards, the rewards of finding out the truth.

On the highway proper Brickman accelerated to seventy, zigzagging around cars on our way to the distant George Washington Bridge. He continually glanced in the rearview mirror. "Are we being followed, Mr. Denny?"

"Of course not," I said. "So why don't we get out at the Seventy-ninth Street exit? We'll go to a coffee shop, have a chat."

"I don't think so, Denny. I think you're going to tell me right now why you're playing these games."

The Rolling Stones were loudly pounding out a

standard. I wondered if my wire could differentiate between Mick Jagger and Thomas Brickman.

"Do you want me to threaten you, Denny?"

"Threaten me?"

We were rapidly gaining on a car when he turned back toward the windshield and swerved around it. Was he threatening me with flying off the road?

"Your fiancée is in my office," he said.

I turned to him. What had he said?

"I think you heard me perfectly, sir."

I looked at his red tie. It was fashioned from fine silk. I looked at his manicured fingernails.

"I'm not kidding," he said.

We sped past the Seventy-ninth Street exit. My heart sometime back had stopped beating.

"We keep all sorts of information on file for birthday greetings, things like that. Sarah referred Mindy Sayles to me. Didn't take long to figure your connection."

"In your office?" I said with a rasp.

"For an urgent checkup. A mammogram. Or whatever my wife told her."

That's why Sarah seemed scared when I called from Boston. Why I got a hang-up this morning.

"Didn't she know you were investigating me?" Brickman said. "I had assumed you'd told her, but I guess you didn't. Seems your secrecy backfired."

I stared at the bridge in the distance. Washington Bridge, Lincoln Tunnel. Denny Dung Heap. "What are you doing with her?" I cried.

"Don't worry," Brickman said, "she's resting comfortably. I gave her a sedative."

"A what!" I grabbed his shoulder. He turned to me, a look of horror in his eyes, as we started, almost in slow motion, to swerve across a lane and a half. A chorus of honking and screeching rubber greeted us as, in a moment that seemed to last forever, he wiggled free of my grasp, turned the steering wheel, and got control of our skid.

I leaned back in my seat. My heart was pounding. A driver in a passing car shouted and made several dozen vulgar gestures while pounding on his horn.

"Look!" From somewhere a pistol appeared in his left hand. "See that?" he said. "Now, settle back. Settle back in your seat."

Settle back. Got it.

"Put your seat belt on. Put it on!"

I clicked it.

"You almost got us killed, Denny. Do you know that? Both of us."

I took a deep breath. I admit it wasn't a rational decision to grab his arm, connected to the steering wheel, at sixty miles per hour.

"Now tell me what you know, Denny. I want to see how effective a risk theorist you are. Tell me what you know! Now!"

"All right," I heard myself saying. "All right."

Trees whipped past the tinted windows. My mind raced with them. I hadn't planned on being threatened in the car. I hadn't planned on his sedating Sarah. I hadn't planned on lots of things.

A good risk assessor predicts all contingencies. A good detective too.

"Start talking, Denny," Brickman said.

I did. In that age-old tradition of Scheherazade, though with a modern slant, with risk theory, odds setting, plus my imaginative powers pumping like mad, I told a story to distract him.

The story of Barry Tenefly, the little engine who could.

There was once an overworked overachiever, I told Brickman, whose father worked very hard in a lumberyard and whose mother died when he was only ten. (I got this information by phone from Tina Nussbaum, daughter of the elder Nussbaum.)

This overworked overachiever remembered his mother with enormous love but also great ambivalence. In fact, after her death he got into lots of trouble, breaking into houses, stealing, fighting. His father tried to beat this out of him with a two-by-four, to no avail.

Oddly the troublemaking ended when the young Tenefly discovered girls. In fact, starting to date, he abruptly stopped making trouble and began overachieving. For three years he got straight A's in his classes, earning a full scholarship to Boston College. Premed there, he again achieved the highest marks.

And then he met Hannah McCory. "Remember Hannah?" I said.

Brickman stared straight ahead. I couldn't read his eyes. I didn't want to read his eyes.

Hannah, a beautiful girl, religiously Catholic, yet from a similar working-class background to Barry's, bewitched the young man. It was hard to say why. Barry went out with girls who knew the ropes, girls who fooled around. Hannah was reclusive, shy, and, even by 1964 standards, a prude.

They went out four times. Four wasn't a charm. On that fourth date, when Hannah denied him a kiss, Barry snapped. And beat and raped her.

Why? Good question. The odds were Brickman would never supply the answer—even if he could.

Barry was arrested and charged with rape and assault. His father hired an expensive and politically connected lawyer who peddled his influence to get a court date with a judge who owed him an enormous favor.

Thus the suspended sentence.

After probation Barry Tenefly disappeared. Tina Nussbaum never saw or heard from him again.

"From there," I said to Brickman, "the rest is conjecture. Conjecture and probability. Risk theory at its imaginative best."

How does one disappear in Massachusetts?

Buzz had told me. You just move to another county and file a petition in probate court to change your name. You don't have to give a reason. With a new name you get a new Social Security number. A new driving license. New everything.

The newly named Thomas Brickman applied to several medical colleges. He only changed the name on the transcripts. The straight A's were real.

At Einstein Medical the overachiever continued to overachieve. After eight years of study he gained success as a doctor specializing in mastectomies and stomach surgery. He married Julie Darrow, got involved in Democratic party politics, and quickly evolved into the American Dream.

"You tell this story well," Brickman said after clearing his throat.

"Wait till you hear the ending," I said.

"I know the ending."

I was betting he didn't.

The overachiever didn't accept the near-cabinet level post in the new administration because there's always a reporter ambitious enough to dig up messy personal stuff. But he felt secure enough to take his own company public.

In fact, the overachiever started thinking he was truly who he pretended to be. Why shouldn't he? Since that April, thirty years ago, he'd done nothing illegal except to tamper with some college transcripts.

And look what he had achieved. Pulled himself

up by his bootstraps. Risen to the top of his profession, to fame and, shortly, wealth. And against colossal odds, odds of tens of thousands to one, millions to one if you factor in the felony that partly strips citizenship and brands one for life like the mark of Cain. Millions to one.

Until one day the odds did a major about-face.

"A new patient made an appointment," I said. "A very inopportune appointment, am I right?"

The chances of this patient's finding Brickman were probably as slim as Brickman's achieving what he had. It required Mindy Sayles to move from Boston into a neighborhood not far from Sarah's. It required accidentally meeting Sarah and discussing personal problems. It required Sarah's knowing Brickman. It required thousands of things, happening precisely as they did. A statistical miracle, a risk theorist might say.

Of course Brickman suspected nothing. He saw women like Mindy every day, women needing mammograms, second opinions, invasive procedures, women angry, afraid, confused, yet ready to trust the famous doctor to steer them to safety.

She was young. Twenty-nine. Rarely do twenty-nine-year-old women, even with lumps, have cancer. Besides, this lump hurt when touched, was hard, and had only recently been discovered. In short, it bore all the telltale signs of a harmless cyst.

But something worried him. Perhaps her staring at his tattoo.

"It's how you played with fate, wasn't it, Brickman?" I said. "Keeping it?"

"What?" Brickman seemed to have been startled awake.

"Keeping it. Betting against the odds that the tattoo would connect you to the past . . . to Barry Tenefly."

Brickman frowned. Obviously he wasn't disclosing to me the building blocks of his logic.

Nor did he disclose to Mindy how familiar her gestures must have seemed, her smile, how she moved, even the way she nervously exposed her breasts. "What part of Boston do you come from?" Thomas Brickman said with a cough.

"Originally South Boston. Do you know Boston?" Mindy had asked.

"I've been there. Done consultations. You can get dressed if you like."

Mindy quickly reclasped the bra and buttoned the blouse. "South Boston in parts is a kind of slum," she said.

"I know." He stared at Mindy's chart. "Is this the correct birthday?" Brickman looked up. "Sometimes patients, for various reasons, change their age—"

Mindy laughed. "Dr. Brickman, I'm still young." She asked the doctor what he thought about the lump.

"You're fine," he said. "It's a cyst."

"Shouldn't I have a mammogram?"

Though it was reasonable for Brickman to recommend against a mammogram for someone so young, women with lumps expect them, especially women whose mothers have died of breast cancer. "Okay, just to be safe," he said, "why don't we do a workup? We'll have something to compare with later on." He scribbled on his prescription paper and told Mindy to take it across the street to Dr. Evans, the radiologist. Mindy took the paper, had the mammogram, and went home.

Despite his original apprehensions, Brickman thought nothing further of this encounter even after receiving a message the next day from the radiologist that Mindy's X rays were positive and a biopsy was required. Three days later Mindy returned to receive anesthesia for the relatively simple in-office procedure. Only when she lay supine on the operating table did Brickman look at a new name added by the nurse to her chart. Mindy's mother's maiden name.

No. Impossible! More impossible? The dates! Brickman madly tried to figure them. My God, it couldn't be . . .

The young anesthesiologist asked if there was something wrong. Brickman stared, uncomprehending. Something wrong? the man repeated. Brickman shook his head. He couldn't stop the surgery; it would arouse suspicion. Besides, he'd done the procedure a thousand times. He could do it in his sleep. He started to cut.

And conflicted, anxious, angry, and scared, his hands shaking, he made an absolute mess. The nurse and the anesthesiologist were amazed. He sloppily, mindlessly scarred her breast.

"Did you intend that? To draw her back?"

"What?"

"Draw her back to you," I said.

"What?" Brickman shouted. He stared at the road. He seemed frightened at his outburst.

Mindy was drawn back, mad as a hatter. She angrily raised her breast from her bra. Near the nipple was a bright red scar, two inches long and a quarter of an inch thick.

"We'll do something about that," Brickman promised.

"What?"

"Plastic surgery. Steroids. You have to realize there are risks."

"Bullshit! You didn't tell me!" she cried, and stamped out of the office. And went to a lawyer, which, as explained, didn't work.

Then Andy Picard stepped in. A sometime boyfriend, he threatened Brickman on the phone. His motives for doing so were unclear, but very clear was his use of Mindy, without her knowledge, as a mule for drugs.

Brickman stared at the bridge in the distance. "What?" he said, startled.

"You didn't know that?" I said. "She carried to clients. Grimes told me she'd switch attaché cases with different stockbrokers. I don't think she knew, but it threw the police completely off. Took you out of the picture."

"They thought it was drugs?" Brickman said, amazed.

"I was the only one who didn't."

Whatever Mindy and Andy Picard were really doing, Brickman didn't want to notify the police or his lawyers. He didn't want anyone to know. So he met Mindy Sayles alone one evening in a public place to ask how much money she wanted. And Mindy started demanding and threatening. And he hit her.

"It just happened, didn't it?" I said. "I'm guessing, but I'll bet from frustration and fear, from all those years, anger roared in you. Was it Jekyll and Hyde? Had you become Barry Tenefly again?"

Brickman glared at me, then turned away.

"That was Sunday," I said. "The next morning you left your office using the back way and drove to her loft. I'm not sure you knew what you wanted to do. But you drove there, didn't you?"

This is what I presumed happened. Just as Brickman arrived, Mindy Sayles raced out and hailed a cab. She'd made an appointment with a risk theorist, Sarah's fiancé. The tan Mercedes followed her cab and stopped and parked at a meter near the Apollo Diner.

"What were you thinking, Brickman, sitting in the car? Your heart must have been pounding. Had you decided? Did you have a plan?"

Somebody had a plan, it seemed, somebody up high. A cabdriver had double-parked and walked into the corner deli. Brickman noticed exhaust from the tailpipe. The cab was running.

And suddenly the door to the Apollo opened and Mindy walked out.

"It must have come together all at once," I said. "The cab with no one in it, Mindy crossing to the kiosk, the heavy traffic on Seventh. I mean, the reality of following her, waiting, the insane, terrible risk you were taking so uncharacteristically. You must have felt you were someone else. Someone you'd been long ago."

Brickman gripped the steering wheel.

"Someone who'd view what was happening as opportunity knocking, opportunity that would come only once and then be gone. Someone who was now telling you to get out of your car and walk to the cab. Which you did. The cab driver with the turban in the deli wasn't watching. You opened the cab door and got in the driver's seat. The keys were there. Your heart must have been racing. You were about to steal some guy's cab. A respected doctor like yourself, about to steal a yellow cab. Your first crime in thirty years! But hardly a crime compared to what was about to happen, was it, Brickman? What had to happen, in your mind, to prevent someone from ruining your life. You couldn't let a woman do that again!"

Brickman seemed in a world of his own.

"For just as Mindy Sayles started to race across Seventh, you stepped on the gas and spun the wheel toward the fruit of your crime. That's

what Mindy Sayles was—wasn't she, Brickman?—
the beautiful fruit from an evil seed. The actual
flowering of your seed, come to haunt you. The
illegitimate daughter of Hannah McCory, begot by
the man who raped her. The rapist! You! Mindy
Sayles was your daughter!"

Brickman suddenly veered across a lane. Luckily we were several car lengths ahead of anyone.

He got back in the lane. Outside, the sunny
Hudson sparkled, but I'm sure Brickman saw a
river of sulfur.

"I didn't think of her as my daughter," Brickman said hoarsely.

"But that's why you killed her. She was living
proof of your crime. Even if she didn't know—and
she didn't—you saw her, even unaware, as a time
bomb. A living, ticking reminder of who you'd
been, there forever to haunt you."

Brickman looked at me. He seemed shocked,
as if what he'd done, repressed, were only now realized.

"She'd ruin everything," Brickman said. "Everything I worked in my life to create. My name,
my family . . ."

"She was your daughter," I cried. "You murdered your daughter!"

"She wouldn't forgive me," Brickman said. "I
killed her because she wouldn't forgive me. If she
found out, she wouldn't forgive me."

Forgive him? What was he talking about? "You
were her father," I said.

Brickman stared ahead, his expression empty. I was in a car with a man who had fallen completely into the void. I was sure of that.

"Well," I said, "she won't forgive you now."

Brickman gripped the steering wheel. I thought for a moment he was finished. All life and fight seemed gone out of him. Just like in the movies, I felt, he was going to drop the pistol and give himself up.

Then he took a sharp breath and looked at me abruptly, as if he'd never seen me before. The bewilderment, fear, even sorrow that had flashed through his eyes was gone. "Finish your story," he said coldly. "I want to hear the ending. Tell me your ending."

So I told him he'd driven the cab of death down Seventh Avenue. He was probably thinking that he'd gotten rid of this weight pulling him back into the past and that again he was free . . . until at Canal Street he noticed smears of red on the windshield. Blood. His daughter's blood.

He parked the cab on North Moore Street. A few passersby must have noticed an elegantly dressed white-haired man exit from the driver's side of a battered yellow cab, but few would recall it. Odd things in New York are kind of relative.

Brickman walked back north to Mindy's loft, a fifteen-minute stroll. There might be evidence in her loft, diaries, newspaper clippings. Perhaps she knew his past and had written letters that, at her death, would reveal the connection. Yes, he was paranoid. After what he had done, who wouldn't be paranoid?

How to get into her loft? He couldn't pick the lock. He hadn't the skills of a private detective.

Fortunately he had the services of one, already there, Dave Washburn of Delaware.

(All the pieces were fitting. All the coincidences, or, as a risk theorist might say, the fluctuations and deviations, were getting stuck into the puzzle and making sense. In the long run.)

Dave Washburn had been assigned a case through the auspices of the Securities and Exchange Commission. Perhaps. Or who was working for some quasi-governmental drug enforcement organization. Perhaps. As these organizations are extremely closemouthed, the real reason for his investigation may never be known.

What is known is that Washburn came to New York intent on phone surveillance and tapped Mindy's phone. Having overheard a phone conversation between her and a man named Dr. Risk, he'd grabbed a cab to the Apollo Diner to eavesdrop in person and during breakfast wrote a cryptic note, hoping to stir something up.

What happened next was bizarre. Outside the young woman got spooked and raced into the street, where a cab crashed into her. Knowing the police would soon descend on her loft, Washburn grabbed a cab back downtown, easily picked the lock, and started mucking around her studio.

On arriving, Brickman didn't know who was inside. It might be Andy Picard, who Brickman had never seen. Brickman slipped in and stooped behind a couch.

Thomas Brickman, cultured physician devoted to healing, would never hurt a fly. Barry Tenefly, blue-collar brawler with a mysterious, vicious temper, could hurt a lot more.

So it was Tenefly who found a glass ashtray, crept up to Washburn, and smashed him on the head. And Tenefly who found a pair of rubber gloves in the kitchen and dragged Washburn into the studio area. He searched Mindy's living area for a half hour, after which, hearing Washburn groan, he raced back to rifle his pockets and take something from around his chest.

On a shelf sat a gallon container of hydrochloric acid. On the floor were several buckets of lead sulfide paint. A doctor certainly knows the potency of hydrogen sulfide and even how to create it.

The snooping man had briefly seen Brickman's face.

"Does it get easier to kill people?" I said. "Is the second easier than the first?"

"Shut up," Brickman said hoarsely. He veered off the highway at the 158th Street exit.

"Where are we going?" I muttered.

The 158th Street exit eventually leads to the Columbia-Presbyterian Hospital complex. But first it circles and twists under an old, disused elevated railroad. If you're not headed for the hospital, there's only one reason to exit here, and that's to create some real mischief. Even with my mind racing, I knew this.

"You haven't finished your story," Brickman said.

I said that eager to take advantage of this new, shady situation, Andy Picard had probably called him. Picard told Brickman of a man named James Denny who had come by, asking questions. How much was it worth to keep his mouth shut about Brickman's connection to Mindy Sayles?

About one bullet, Brickman had decided, for at the loft he'd taken Dave Washburn's pistol and shoulder holster (Grimes had overlooked the possibility of a private detective's carrying a licensed pistol). Meeting Andy Picard in the street near Mindy's loft, he shot Picard point-blank in the forehead.

We bounced over cobblestones. Overhead you could hear the whir of highway traffic. The commotion would drown out a gun shot. Not that anyone would care about the sound of a gunshot here.

Brickman steered to a stop among several abandoned cars in various states of dismemberment, a graveyard of rubber and steel. Not my graveyard, I swore.

"Don't you want to hear more?" I said.

Among several rusted, slaughtered automobiles, Brickman put the gear in park and stared at me.

"There's another part to the story," I continued frantically. I assumed Brickman's plan was to shoot me outside the car. No blood and guts on his upholstery. Thus my plan not to get out of the car unless I had to. My overall plan, which in theory had once seemed bulletproof, was making me incredibly nervous. "The person who chased me by the piers?" I continued. "My first thought? One of Picard's boys. Or someone you'd hired. But you hadn't hired anyone. You didn't trust anyone. You came in a mustache and beret yourself, like Halloween. Over the edge, in broad daylight, to shoot me."

"Get out of the car," Brickman said.

I grabbed the door handle. Slowly, so slowly I opened it without a click. "Detective Grimes knows it's you," I said. "I told him you were picking me up. Forensics will tie you to this."

"I don't think so, Denny," Thomas Brickman said. "I think you're in this all by yourself. You're living some adolescent fantasy."

Brickman was either a clairvoyant or a psychoanalyst with a Viennese degree. "What are you saying, Brickman?" I asked.

"I'm saying that I know what it's like."

"What?"

"Not to be what you want. And to live a fantasy and want it so bad you'll do anything to make it real."

"What are you talking about?"

"Who you are, Mr. Denny. Who we are."

And suddenly I knew what had drawn me to

Thomas Brickman. We both were made of the same cloth: overachievers trying to achieve what we couldn't.

Except Brickman *had* achieved his persona. And I and my tough-guy, private eye fantasy were right now going down the tubes.

"You're about a mile over your head, aren't you, Denny? A risk assessor who took too big a risk. You should have stuck to writing your little column instead of living the risks in them. Get out of the car."

"No one will believe you, Brickman," I said, not budging. In the car he wouldn't shoot me. I was betting my life on that.

"To the contrary. When the police run up against the dead wall of my alibi, they'll recall a man chasing you on the piers. That will be the connection. Not me."

"You killed your daughter," I said. "Stop the killing."

"I never thought of her as my daughter. She was only genetically—"

I burst out the door.

This much I knew: I had five seconds to be alive or dead. My plan, based on his strategy— game theory, come on—was that he'd hesitate to fire through his windows. And this happened. I heard no shot.

He had to get out his side, and that would take three to four seconds. I heard his door open. I got into the middle of the street and started running.

The shot echoed like thunder under the disused railroad, but I felt nothing. Then there was an explosion in my back, like someone hitting me with a two-by-four. I got shot forward and stumbled, but I didn't stop moving.

I was wearing body armor purchased from Richie at the Spying Store! Zepel-treated, urethane-coated, lightweight, rip-stop nylon strapped around my chest. According to Richie, it should stop mid-caliber bullets at a range of ten yards. The farther away and the smaller the caliber, the very much better as, up close, though bulletproof, the vest wasn't fatal-proof (the trauma from impact can kill you).

Richie had quizzed me on the gunshot sounds at the pier (tinny, high-pitched) and the splinters of wood (thin, fragmented). In Brickman's hand the barrel looked small, low-caliber. Wonderful, I thought. Things were working as planned!

Only my back was killing me despite the rip-stop nylon. It felt as if somebody had plunged a steak knife in. My sprint had deteriorated into a clumsy, painful lope. Brickman would catch me in a snap.

I looked over my shoulder. He wasn't after me! He'd gotten back in the car. Something had spooked him. He's driving away!

Brickman drove, but not away.

At such moments you're supposed to dig down deep into your character to find that extra effort and energy to pull you up from the brink. I dug deep into my fervent desire not to be a corpse. I grabbed a girder and pulled myself around just as the Mercedes roared past. I heard it screech to a stop. I followed the line of the girder as another pistol shot cracked. Another clang as bullet hit steel.

Risk assessing and game theory had now gone the way of the buggy whip. Indeed, my formalized training couldn't come up with any advice more effective than "Keep your head down!" I moved and jumped and ducked from a sixth sense that had more affinity to a cat than a man.

I flattened myself against a junked taxi without wheels or windows and listened to my heartbeats, a reassuring sound; I still had heartbeats. I stuck my head up. Brickman pointed the pistol. Steel and rust went flying!

I crawled around another vehicle. The din from the highway above helped hide my noisy maneuvering. At the back of a junked van I saw, back to me, uncertain for an instant, Brickman. Well, it was now or never.

"What?" Brickman cried as I raced toward him. I didn't hear the shot, but felt it, to the right of my chest, a glancing shot . . . Glancing? A blowtorch got turned up at my rib cage!

I screamed and closed my arm and elbow on Brickman's hand.

My little tai chi master has said again and again, nine years straight, "Turning saves your life." Meaning all of tai chi's power and leverage and torque get generated from circles and turns. With Brickman's hand caught under my arm, and without a second even to debate the matter, I turned. I didn't do anything else, just turned quickly, and all my body parts and joints turned with me, pivoting around the small of my back.

I broke his wrist.

At least I think I did. I heard a snap and a surprised cry, and Brickman held up his hand, no pistol in it. The hand seemed violently disconnected from the wrist, just hanging there attached by a flap of skin. Brickman stared, horrified, at his newly configured appendage.

Physician, I felt like saying, heal thyself.

The gun clattered to the cobblestones. I kicked it hard, and it slid somewhere under these junked automobiles. Then I turned back, more turning, and the turning forcibly shoved Brickman against the side of an open windshield and, as luck would have it, for I couldn't have timed this if I tried, right back into my clenched fist. His Roman nose smeared across his face, blood spurted, and he was out, just like that. He slumped down into the gutter.

I decided to sum up what I was doing, have a little dialogue with myself, a little swift psychodrama, as my mind was racing. So, I thought, *James, you've done it. The madman is in a coma, breathing loudly through his broken schnozz. The gun's inaccessible. You're probably alive, though you can't be certain. You have to feel, see if all the organs are intact. Okay, there are no holes in the vest near your chest, just a kind of numbness that'll wear off with adrenaline and hurt like death. The odds are good you're in one piece.*

Now what? You're in the middle of Harlem; you can hardly walk; every time your heart beats it's like a horse kicking you in the chest. Plus there isn't a phone within several blocks of here, and you're right next to a brand-new Mercedes. Wouldn't that be a riot, after cheating death à la Brickman, to get mugged and stabbed by a gang of car thieves?

I decided to look for the gun.

Let me say this: Pain is entirely relative. What I now felt crawling on my hands and knees, compared with before, was even worse. I almost puked from the pain. Comatose Brickman, I was also certain, would at any second revive and metamorphose into a bionic terminator ready to spring up and crush me. So, having found the pistol in a puddle under a decaying Buick, I took a relaxing breath.

Even that hurt.

A phone? Thank you, Mercedes! Groaning with every step, and thanking my memory for not entirely lapsing, I made my way to that lush interior and Brickman's car phone, which I'd forgot about. I called Grimes at the precinct.

"Lieutenant Grimes," I moaned when a woman answered.

"Who's this?"

I mentioned my name and was told to hold on.

I waited ten seconds, long enough to decide to hell with them. To hell with . . .

"Dr. Risky?" I heard.

"What?"

"It's Lowery. Where the hell are you?"

I told him as best I could.

"Hold on, we're getting a squad car out there."

"Brickman's here," I said.

I heard shouting on the other end of the line.

"Risky?" Lowery said. "Everything's going to be all right."

"Send an ambulance. My fiancée," I mumbled.

"She's covered," Lowery cried, and hung up.

Covered? With a winding sheet? No, she was just sedated. I started to call Brickman's office to make sure when I turned. Brickman! Where was he?

He'd slumped down a little farther. Amazing. He looked so peaceful lying there, like a child, and I imagined in this weird moment, for some reason I'm still not sure of, the long-ago Barry Tenefly, before any of this happened, the rape, the struggle, the climb up the ladder, and then the murders and the tumbling all the way back down. Barry Tenefly, the boy, dreaming of being Thomas Brickman. Barry Tenefly, the man-child, filled with far-flung hopes and dreams.

And thinking this, I partly identified with the overachiever. I had been trying to accomplish a farfetched dream myself. I had tried to climb a ladder toward a strange ambition, to overachievement, and it seemed I'd succeeded. Would I wind up like Brickman, who'd reached for the stars but fell to the depths?

Thinking this, I felt, well, a little sorry for him. Then I remembered Mindy, and feeling sorry completely disappeared.

Something dripped from the elevated railway above me. Water, I guessed. It splashed on the windshield. Things dripped, even here, meaning there was gravity, meaning I was still on terra firma. Still alive and kicking. I noticed beyond the moist gloom of this auto graveyard under the disused railway the blue-green Hudson, its small waves glittering from yellow sunlight. I felt like walking from the gloomy darkness into that sunshine while singing the praises of life, liberty, and the pursuit of happiness. I felt like praising Allah, Yahweh, and any other god I could think of. I felt like reveling in the philosophy of a loaf of bread, a jug of wine, and not thou, Brickman. Not thou.

The dripping water beat Chinese torture on the windshield until the sirens got louder.

CHAPTER
25

I got to ride in an ambulance. You'd think that would be fun, riding up front, the siren whirring, watching traffic and people scurrying out of the way. But I was in the rear, flat on my back, strapped to a stretcher, my view the rusting ceiling and a couple of straps on hooks bouncing a lot over my head. You would think the suspension in one of these vehicles would be ratcheted up a notch to lower the risks of an injured invalid like myself getting whacked around like a rag doll. No. Every bump, cobblestone, and pothole got hammered onto my ribs, as if God Almighty were angrily communicating to me in visceral Morse code.

Luckily Columbia-Presbyterian was just ten blocks away.

Dr. Thomas Brickman was somewhere not far behind in his own private ambulance, with two NYPD police as traveling buddies. They wanted his company so badly they'd handcuffed his remaining good hand to the stretcher to make sure he didn't accidentally wander off.

The EMS boys had tried to tear off the voice-activated wire from my chest, but I clung to that. I wanted to deliver that personally.

About an hour later in my semiprivate hospital room I did.

I'd just got propped up on one of those high-tech hospital beds when Lieutenant Grimes walked in. Grimes wore a big blue Windbreaker with a yellow POLICE stenciled neatly onto the back. He looked really professional in that. I reminded myself to compliment him on it later. Much later.

"You okay?" he asked.

"No thanks to you," I said softly. Speaking loudly, I discovered, also hurt.

"James," Grimes said.

What the hell, I decided to be big about this, until I could get up and do something to him personally. I motioned briefly to a chair beside the bed. Grimes sat down and looked around the room. Across from us an old man slept in a closed-off hospital bed, beside which were several bouquets of flowers. I hadn't been here long enough to get my area nice and homey. "I don't blame you for not getting my message," I said bitterly, trying not to cough. Coughing also hurt. "I didn't give you much lead time."

"I was out in the field, James," Grimes said plaintively.

"Right," I said. "You were out in the field while I was getting the shit kicked out of me. Why didn't you listen?"

"James, I listened."

"Baloney."

"I got your prints."

I stared.

"I called in my favor at the commissioner's office, Boston way," Grimes said. "They unsealed Tenefly's file and got the Police Department to send me the prints. I got Brickman's here, and they matched."

"Why didn't you tell me?" I cried out. That also hurt.

"Didn't get it till this morning. Man, you're so impatient. When I made the match, I was busy getting your lady friend."

I moved the wrong way. That might also have hurt like crazy, but my feelings were pounding elsewhere. "Got her?"

Grimes explained. Being in the field meant entering Brickman's office with a search warrant just about the time the good doctor picked me up for that lovely car ride. And getting Julie Brickman to tell immediately about the sedative, not a problem, as she felt certain her husband was betraying her by hiding a mistress, or worse.

Much worse.

"Where's Sarah?"

"They're checking her out in ER. She's okay, but Brickman shot her up with lots of crap."

"That fuck," I said forcefully, and regretted that.

Grimes winced along with my wincing. "They've got Brickman on the next floor. Operating room. Doctors are working on his wrist. You did some job, James. What do you know, martial arts?"

"Tai chi. No risk." If you also wear a rip-stop nylon vest. "Did he confess?" I said with a rasp.

Grimes stared. "James, his fancy lawyers'll do the talking."

"Not this time, Lieutenant," I said, and with a little flourish held up the tiny, voice-activated recorder. "Do you accept taped confessions?" I asked.

Grimes stared at me. I pressed the button, and we listened to Bruce Springsteen singing and in the background myself saying, "She was your daughter. You murdered your daughter!"

"She wouldn't forgive me," Brickman said. "I killed her because she wouldn't forgive me."

I clicked the recorder shut, ejected the tape, and handed it to Grimes, who held it gingerly like a fine piece of crystal too expensive even to think of dropping. Grimes stared some more. "James," he finally said after a cough.

"What?

"I misjudged you."

"Misjudged me?"

He looked around. He stared at his shoes. "Didn't think . . . " he mumbled.

"Lieutenant, I can't hear you."

"Didn't think," he said louder, "you were tough enough to take real heat. To take real chances."

"And now you do?" I said. "Should I glow warmly inside?"

Grimes's eyes lit up, in anger or delight.

Well, I had kind of doubted this myself. I had doubted my ability to take risks instead of assessing them in safety. To live life instead of watching it fly past. Which is what you've got to do to figure out the crime. Get in there up to your elbows, to get at the truth.

We looked at each other a moment, the detective and I.

Grimes asked how I'd figured out Mindy was Brickman's daughter.

"Risk theory," I said. "I used a fault tree."

"Fault tree?"

Though the odds of successfully explaining this to Grimes seemed tiny, I continued. "A fault tree is a risk theory device. You start with a disaster and go backward toward the truth."

"The truth?" Grimes said.

"Brickman's motive. What I needed and never could guess. Because I never assumed he'd run from what he was. What he'd done. I never assumed his greatest disaster was his past. You see, Lieutenant, in risk theory all risks are relative. You take small risks to avoid great ones. It's all a trade-off."

"Trade-off?"

"Brickman traded off his present safety to quash the fear of his past. He was truly scared of that. That's where we were different."

"What are you talking about, James?" Grimes said, looking askance.

"Lieutenant, did you know how hooked I was on this guy? How much I had Brickman-on-my-mind?"

"Oh, did I know, James."

"But I didn't know why until I realized we were kind of the same. We both wanted to be different from what we were. He wanted to be a respected, wealthy doctor, the opposite of what he'd been. I wanted to be a tough private eye, the opposite of—"

"James," Grimes said, holding up the tiny tape and smiling, "you are."

"I'm not tough."

Grimes's grin grew wider. "Tough sounds good to me."

Was this some kind of mutual admiration society? Tough is to the beholder?

Tough? Maybe I was.

"Anyway, he hated who he was," I said. "He ran from who he was. He was ashamed of it."

"And you?" Grimes asked.

"I was running away. I wasn't living my life."

"Sounds like you two were peas in a pod," Grimes said with a grin.

"No," I said. "We were different. We were very different."

"How so?"

I thought of Julie Brickman and Mindy Sayles and Hannah McCory. We were different.

"Well, James," Grimes said after a pause, "I'm very impressed."

"Some of this assessing was purely luck," I added, remembering Sister Cary. "Luck and the long run."

"Uh-oh. You're talking about the long run again?"

I smiled broadly. "Lieutenant, I told you in the long run risk theory works like a charm. The odds come out precisely. With Brickman too. All the deviations, fluctuations, coincidences, in the long run, fitted exactly and made sense."

"You mean the past caught up with the guy?" Grimes said.

I stared. Amazing how, without a clue, this nonrisk theorist could hit the nail on the head.

Risk theory had righteously caught up with Thomas Brickman. You see, in the coveted long run, the odds balance out. Which kind of sums up this risk theorist's definition of justice. What goes around comes around, you reap what you sow—homilies that are in a way the guts of risk theory.

In the long run Hannah McCory's suffering had

caught up with Barry Tenefly, the man who had caused it. And swept him into a dustbin of fury.

All, of course, with a little help from me.

"What I don't understand," I said, "is what Brickman meant when he said she wouldn't forgive him. He said, 'I killed her because she wouldn't forgive me.'"

"Yeah, I heard that," Grimes said.

"What did he mean? She was his own daughter, his flesh and blood. She might have forgiven him. Unless," I said, "he meant someone else."

"Someone else?"

"Not his daughter."

"His wife?"

"Someone in his past. Someone who died when he was very young. His mother died when he was ten. Maybe he meant she wouldn't forgive him."

Grimes stared at me.

"Lieutenant, to a ten-year-old, a mother dying might seem to be a major act of unforgiveness. On her part. For some imagined offense."

"James?"

"What?"

"They giving you the right drugs?"

I had to smile. "Well, we'll probably never know, will we, Lieutenant? So there'll be a page missing to this mystery."

"James, this is real life."

"I know," I said. "I like that. I like that fine."

Grimes stared at me and stood. He coughed. "You need anything?" he said.

I was going to say "a few new ribs," but didn't. I winked. Boy, was I a tough guy or what?

"I'll look in on you later," Grimes said.

"Lieutenant, I'm fine."

Then I heard, "Where is he? Is James Denny there?"

"Is that Sarah?" I whispered. Oh, no. "Lieutenant, tell her I'm sleeping."

Grimes started grinning. "Now, haven't you finished fibbing to her yet?"

"I can't tell her the truth now," I whispered. I felt terribly guilty, obviously, that she'd got involved in this, that she'd almost gotten seriously hurt, but now was just the wrong time.

"How about I tell her the truth?" Grimes said.

"No, no, you can't, Lieutenant!"

But Grimes had already left the room. I heard Sarah greet him. I heard Grimes say I wanted to tell her something but was weighing the risks.

"The risks?" Sarah cried.

"Long-run and short-run risks," Grimes said. "Long run and short run he's up the creek."

"I don't understand. James? Are you there? Are you all right?"

I girded myself for the enormous and terrifying risks of . . . a relationship.